Canal Murder

First paperback edition printed in 2021 in the United Kingdom

A catalogue record for this book is available from the British Library

ISBN
Paperback 978-1-915742-29-2
Kindle 978-1-915742-28-5

Published by The Creative Peak(TCP)

Book Design: T M Goble
Cover Image: Copyright Shutterstock

T M Goble's Website

www.tmgoble.com

Action Thrillers
Detective Murder Mysteries
Standalone Murder Mysteries
Historical Fiction
Contemporary Fiction
History of Peak District Literature
Seasonal Recipes
I occasionally send newsletters with details on new releases, special offers and other bits of news relating to my books.

Day One

01

It has been a long time since I attended the office, but my editor wants a face-to-face meeting which is unusual. I give a final check to my appearance in the mirror of the ladies' toilet. My new grey trouser suit complements a blue cashmere jumper. My appearance is business-like, which pleases me. I press my lips together and apply a smear of pale pink lip gloss. I repress the urge to do a twirl in front of the mirror. Why am I feeling so light-hearted?

With a bounce in my step, and a smile on my face, I stride along the corridor. Since the last time, a complete refurbishment has been accomplished and the editor is now in a new office. In the past meetings with him have often been delayed for hours because of major difficulties on the newspaper, but I can't complain if it occurs today, as he runs the most popular of the broadsheets and pays me well. Approaching the half glass door, I give a gentle tap. As I wait, I tilt my head to one side and listen for a response.

'Come!'

I thrust the door open and step inside. The office is much bigger than his previous one which had been rather poky. This one is more stylish, with sleek modern furniture and a colourful abstract print on the wall. Not to my taste but it does add a splash of colour to the room. Jumping up from his desk he nips around and envelops me in an enthusiastic embrace. It's his usual style. It is not only the office that is different. His normally dishevelled hair is now neatly trimmed and as far as I can remember he has never worn a tweed jacket. The green textured fabric with a leather collar and cuffs is complemented by a black turtleneck sweater. My first thought is that it's a fresh image to complement his pristine office, but I brush the idea aside. Perhaps there is a new woman in his life. That idea is much more interesting. What a pity I can't ask him. It is far too impertinent.

Instead, I opt for a bland comment, 'Smart jacket, Toby.'

His eyes glint with amusement. 'The new air conditioning is freezing. I yearn for the old hot and humid conditions.' Opening his hand for me to sit in front of the desk, he returns to his smart cream leather chair, where he swivels to and fro for a few moments before speaking. 'We are struggling for copy which is why I have asked you to come in. I can fill the paper but there will be no headline that will capture the reader's attention. Did you read through the case notes that I sent you?'

'Yes, a miscarriage of justice is my type of assignment, but the details are sketchy, so the investigation will need time and effort and I am already covering two other columns for the next few weeks.'

He extracts a sheet of paper from a drawer and with a flourish, places it on his desk and pushes it towards me. 'This was in this morning's paper. Did you see it?'

I read it. *Amanda Mallory will investigate the death in the London churchyard two years ago. Was it the biggest miscarriage of justice in England's history? Discover the secrets she has unearthed next week.*

I reread the words to assure myself I have not made a mistake. No. I resist the urge to wave my arms about in a wild manner and to use all the swear words in my repertoire. With restraint I keep my hands firmly grasped in my lap as I stare in astonishment. 'Bloody hell, Toby. That's ridiculous. The time is too short. I won't get appointments for weeks with the interested parties and you know the police won't cooperate. It cannot be done.' My blood boils when he makes these ridiculous decisions that put me under pressure. I try to gather my thoughts and pretend that I am calm, although I am seething at his preposterous suggestion in such a short time scale.

Ignoring my words, he pushes a file across the table towards me, 'I wanted to help, so the overnight team have put together more information. It's short notice, Amanda, but you always come up with the goods. Your investigative skills are superb.'

I flick my hand at him as I am in no mood to pander to his hints of flattery, 'Don't give me that rubbish. The whole idea is ridiculous. The answer is no. The deadline is far too soon.'

'Do your best.' Smiling, he swings his chair to the side, pushes himself to his feet and walks across the room to pick up his coat from the clothes peg in the corner.

Initially his movements confuse me but as he dons his smart overcoat, it's obvious he is leaving. 'What's going on? Where are you going?' I blurt out in a sharp voice. 'We need to discuss this assignment.'

'Haven't time, I've an important meeting at Heathrow.'

With a cheery wave of his hand, he hurries out of his office, leaving me sitting on my own. How dare he flounce out of the meeting as though he hasn't a care in the world. I bang my fist on his desk in frustration making the table lamp sway alarmingly. I place it back in its original position. It's obvious that I have no alternative but to accept this assignment if I want to continue to earn good money.

Taking a deep breath, I remain in the empty office as I ponder the details of the murder. It was a case that had piqued my interest when I'd read through the notes, but I would encounter a lot of resistance from the legal profession and the police. The poor lass has already been in jail for two years. Aged eighteen she had received a life sentence for murder. The big man she murdered was a slob who often slept in the churchyard. She tended the flowers in the church and was special needs with a reading age of eight. The solicitor had advised her to plead guilty. Why?

02

The invitation to a party this evening on a neighbouring boat, is propped on the small bookshelf. Its over flamboyant style irritates me, making it appear phoney. I frown in confusion at my thoughts. Why do I think that? Jasmine, our neighbour, has gone over the top with the invite. It's just her usual style. Afterall, she is an artist, and that explains a great deal. The background print on the A4 invitation reminds me of the style of Constable at Flatford Mill, but the painting is a modern scene from along the canal at Little Venice. Perhaps her artistic mind has blended the two scenes that are centuries apart.

Across the print, the invite is scribed in her flamboyant hand. Why does it appear false? I couldn't come up with an idea. As an amateur painter, although my mind's eye of the scene never transfers to the canvas, I usually appreciate creativity. But not on this occasion, although I have to acknowledge that Jasmine is undoubtably talented.

I've known her for two years, but we have never become best friends. We enjoy a cup of coffee and a chat occasionally but that's about it. She lives on the canal boat next to ours with her partner, Benjamin, who is a successful author. When we relocated from our small cramped flat in central London, we chose to buy a narrow boat with mooring facilities on Regent's Canal. It was a more affordable option and I had this romantic notion of living in a small creative community on the canal. It's close enough to the city, and also my dad who lives nearby, but was a chance to live in a more relaxed environment. Our small community has four boats and on the whole we all muddle along together reasonably well.

Sitting on the stern deck, soaking up a little of the weak sunshine with a large cup of coffee, my mind drifts back to my investigative assignment. I try to shake off the panic which surfaces every time I think about it. In my heart of hearts, I know the task is impossible but I shall have to gather some inner reserves of determination to complete the assignment.

Pushing the anxious thoughts aside I focus on the evening ahead. The weather is dry and fairly warm which is a relief as we will be able to use the area on the tow path. Squeezing everyone into the limited space on a narrow boat is tricky and such a crush would spoil the ambience of the party. It is still an hour before the merrymaking commences. The stated timing is immaterial, as other people's adherence to the clock means nothing to Jasmine, who tends to drift through her artistic day oblivious to other people's regimes.

Arriving at the specified time is an obsession of mine so I keep a careful eye on the clock. It's surprising how quickly time flies when you are relaxing and enjoying a well-earned rest. As yet I haven't made a final decision about what to wear. It all depends on what takes my fancy after I've showered. My husband, Jason is laid back and goes with the flow, and I doubt if he will even change his clothes for the party. His usual attire of sweatshirt and jeans are acceptable for a social evening on a canal boat. Not that he changes his appearance often. He is getting into a rut.

Rufus, our German Shepherd, moves position and flops down on my feet. Smiling, I will allow him ten minutes as this is always his chosen spot. It's a strange position, but if it makes him happy, that's okay by me. Even if I fidget, he never seems to mind. Patting him as his large head is close to my knee, he lazily wags his tail and lifts his head to stare at me with his large brown eyes. He is such a lovely dog. He is a monster compared to those we meet on our walks, wanting to play boisterously and to bark with a little too much enthusiasm. But he and I have an understanding. How that has developed, I have never fully understood, so we relax together and enjoy the early evening sunshine. Living on a narrowboat suits me. It is calming and relaxing. Perhaps it's living close to the water. Whatever it is I have enjoyed it ever since our first day on *Serendipity*. At the beginning the novelty of calling the kitchen, a galley, and the lounge a salon was great fun. Living in such a confined space is perfect, although a minimalistic approach is sensible. Too much clutter is not suitable and everything must earn its space. Closing my eyes, I listen to the gently lapping water as I enjoy the moment and lift my face towards the warming sunshine.

The person approaching on the towpath catches my attention. What is he doing here? As he wanders along, studying the canal boats, I wait for him to reach the point on the towpath where he will be able to see and hear me.

I wave my arm in a frantic gesture to catch his attention. I don't want to move as this will disturb Rufus. 'Toby, what a surprise. I've never seen you here before.'

He stands with his hands on his hips as his dark snappy eyes flit across the boat. This afternoon his face has a strange expression which is difficult to fathom. 'Amanda, I know we met this morning, but I've been searching for you, although I did not know that you lived on a canal boat until I looked up your address in the office. Canal boats do not go in sequence, so you were difficult to locate.'

'Come on board, but be careful, as it is a big step to the stern. Hold on to the mooring rope as the boat can rock with passing traffic.'

Gingerly, he begins to step down.

Rufus growls. As usual it is low and menacing.

'Rufus! Stay.' Toby stops halfway and eyes Rufus with apprehension. 'It's okay. He's just letting you know that this is his territory.'

Toby sidles onto the seat opposite to me on the rear stern while watching Rufus. He attempts to relax as Rufus flops over my feet once again with a sigh.

For the first time, I study his face which is solemn and anxious? That is unusual for Toby. Confident and assured is his normal style.

'What's up, Toby? It is a surprise visit, but you are most welcome and you can stay as the next boat is having a party this evening.'

Shaking his head, he chews on his bottom lip while his face remains pensive. 'I have come to talk to you about a message that arrived in the office early this afternoon, although I do not regard it seriously.'

He remains silent for a few moments as he stares at Rufus with an expression of discomfort. 'You've lost me and need to elaborate.' This has happened on numerous occasions. His mind is fast thinking, and few can keep pace with him, but I need him to be succinct, as I must dress for the party. My eye flicks to the clock. I still have enough time.

'Sorry, Amanda. I'm a little distracted. Because it is important, I wanted to inform you personally.'

Why is he here? He always texts and if crucial he will ring me. Something unusual must have happened.

Appearing to regather his thoughts, he transfers his attention from Rufus to me.

He rubs a hand across his face. Before speaking he lets out a long slow sigh. 'This afternoon we received an anonymous death threat directed at you.'

'What!' I shriek, as a stab of terror hits me in the gut. Rufus growls as though to add his concern. 'Why haven't you contacted me earlier? Bloody hell, this is important.' I am breathing heavily in an attempt to control the panic that threatens to engulf me. 'It warrants far more than a meander along the canal on the chance of tracking down the boat.' My voice rises to a point of hysteria.

Rufus lifts his head and lets out a more ominous deep growl, as though his displeasure to the proceedings is increasing. Toby slinks back in his seat.

Needing to know far more information without Rufus's assistance, I place my hand on his head to calm him. It stops him from growling. My stomach twists, my face flushes and I have a furtive glance along the tow path to ensure there is no one lurking nearby. Someone is threatening to kill me. Bloody hell. This is no laughing matter. I command myself to remain calm but it is impossible. Should I call Jason? He should know of any threats to me.

Rufus whimpers.

'Settle, fella.' I stroke his ear, but he remains alert. Has he sensed my nervousness?

Returning my direct gaze to Toby, 'For goodness sake, enlighten me, I need to know all the details.' I force the words from my mouth in a hurried almost frenzied manner.

'There is little information, which is why the police are not concerned, but they intend to follow it up. We received the message on the usual public site where people can inform us of any incidents.'

My stomach wants to rebel but gulping restores some equilibrium. 'What did it say?'

Rufus whimpers. I pat him.

'Do not pursue the case of the dead man in the churchyard, otherwise the reporter will join her.'

It is not as bad as I anticipate as it only mentions the reporter, but my name was blazoned over the front page this morning.

'The police have all the details, but they expect it to be a nutter.'

Although I have a modicum of relief about the indirect reference, Toby has taken time to find and tell me which means he thinks it's important. I gulp at his concern. Although quivering from the news, I attempt to remain calm.

My investigative journalist colleagues on other newspapers and television, receive death threats as they often delve into serious current crimes, such as drug running. They appear to take it in their stride, but I only ever deal with old cases of injustice. I regard myself as a coffee table journalist exposing past wrongs. Death threats are not part of the job.

03

After Toby's departure I sit quietly thinking through the death threat. At the earliest opportunity, I shall visit dad and discuss the matter with him. After all he was a police inspector before his retirement and can advise me on the best approach.

The clumping sound coming through the boat alerts me to Jason's imminent arrival. Scowling, he appears in the stern seating area wearing his usual crocs. His dishevelled appearance is the norm these days. Where is the smart energetic man that I married? Rufus lifts his head but is disinterested and wriggles to make himself more comfortable on my feet.

'Who were you talking to? I've not seen him before.'

'Bloody hell, Jason, are you losing the plot? You have met him several times but being in your own distant world you choose not to recognise my friends and colleagues.'

With a nonplussed expression he ignores my comments and peers across towards *Carpe Diem*, the boat moored next to us, where Jasmine is putting up the bunting ready for the party. Slumping on the bench, he rakes a hand through his untidy hair and his limp posture suggests apathy. I allow the silence to stretch as I contemplate him. Keeping his eyes fixed on Jasmine he rolls his shoulders, 'Why are you in a bad mood?'

I grip the cushions next to me as my frustration rises. For some reason I don't tell him about the death threat. In his current mood I doubt that he will show any interest. Although we have been married nearly twenty years, his attitude in recent months is becoming more dismissive.

Jasmine continues to hold his attention. Her tight shorts and cropped top expose a substantial amount of skin, but she likes the attention from men and I'm sure she dresses that way deliberately. To be fair she does have a slender figure which she enhances in every way possible. If I was being unkind, I'd say she was a flirt. After being on the boat next to her for two years she has become a slight friend but it will never develop into a serious friendship, as we do not have enough in common.

Staring across at him, I guess that he has come to wheedle some money out of me, so he can buy drinks for the party. When Jason needs cash, as I am the big money earner between us, he implies that my irritation with him is because I am approaching the menopause. But his logic confounds me. If he wants money, then why alienate me, but the trend has been obvious for a long time and has increased with venom in the last few months.

Curling his lip, 'You aren't ready for the party.' I do not like the bitter tone of his voice. What is happening to him? Doesn't he possess any pleasant manners?

Biting my lip, he appears to be dressed in clothes that have been dragged from the canal. He has never been the most fashionable dresser but has sunk to new levels recently.

'Of course, I'm not bloody ready for the party. I've been busy. If you leave me in peace for a while, I will shower and dress.' He has annoyed me several times a day in recent months. This can't continue. We must have a serious chat and he needs to find a job and earn some money. It was never my intention to be the sole wage earner.

'I'll fetch wine from the off-licence unless you have bought some.'

'No, I haven't.' There is no point in escalating his lack of doing anything useful. I need the party and a few gins to calm down from the news that Toby had imparted. It worries me that I have received a death threat.

Staring at me, he transfers his attention to my handbag, indicating that he wants money. The hassle is not worth it tonight. Opening my bag, I flick him my credit card. 'Don't just buy cheap wine, get me a bottle of the decent gin.'

With a mundane facial expression, he picks up the card without any acknowledgement or thanks. Stepping up from the stern of the boat to the towpath, he waves and calls out to Jasmine with a smile.

04

Jason plods away at his usual slow pace along the towpath. There is no energy in his movements. Totally lazy is the thought that springs into my mind. Will our marriage last? We argue practically every time we meet, and he avoids me whenever possible. I nibble at my lip as my eyes fill with tears. Rarely will I seek him out and most conversations have degenerated into one word snapped responses. I don't want to split with him but it's time to clear the air between us. Such a discussion needs to occur soon. I should have done it months ago, but with no heart for it, I delayed.

To make matters worse he ogles other women far more. It has become embarrassing. The expression on his face as he stared at Jasmine putting up the bunting spoke volumes. We must speak seriously. He never stares at me with any desire these days. I'm just as good looking as Jasmine. Like her, I have long blonde hair and a good figure. Walking with Rufus twice a day keeps me trim and in good shape. But in Jason's eyes I'm just the money earner.

Wiping my eyes, I no longer want to go to the party. My mood has plummeted, but perhaps the gin, if he remembers to buy some at the off-licence, will improve my attitude to my marriage and push the death threat to the back of my mind.

Jasmine finishes the bunting and turns her attention to the barbecue. It has a steel base with a large bowl for the charcoal. With the metal grill on the top, it will produce poor quality burgers for the evening.

I close my eyes as the silly woman does not have a clue about setting it up. Why hasn't Benjamin come to help her?

Moving Rufus from my feet, I jump up the steps to the towpath. It's obvious that she hasn't thought things through so I'll give her a bit of assistance.

Wandering towards her, I give a friendly smile, 'You can't set that up there, Jasmine. It's blocking the path.'

Curling her lip, she glowers, 'It looks all right to me.' My suggestion has not been well received. The fact that it might inconvenience other people by obstructing the tow path is irrelevant to her.

I try a different tack, 'Where's Benjamin. Isn't he helping you?'

Shrugging, 'He never bloody helps. I do it all on my own. The barbecue is staying there.'

I'd come from the boat with the intention of helping her, but with that type of attitude she must sort out her own problems.

I flap a hand at the offending object, 'It's blocking the bloody path.'

'I don't care.'

A bad habit, that I have always had, is wanting the last word and I normally choose something scathing. I've had a bad day, so I cannot contain myself. 'You wanted the party. I am sure Benjamin didn't. Therefore, you can expect to do the work. Don't blame me if an irate walker or dog owner pushes the damned barbecue into the canal.'

Without waiting for a reply, I stomp back to the *Serendipity*. By the time I step onto the stern deck, I regret my outburst. I will give it twenty minutes, then go to apologise. With tears of frustration, I head for the galley to fix myself a gin and tonic as I need one. Then I dump myself on the stern seating to sip it and wait for my annoyance to settle. Rufus flops on my feet again.

05

Trying to persuade Rufus his sleep time is over can be an uphill task. I pat him and tickle his ears. Finally, he responds and moves from my feet. As I stand and stretch, Abigail is wandering along the towpath. I had hoped she would come to the party as the other boat owners like her, but she has reached the age in her first year in Uni that her parents' parties are now a thing of the past.

I shudder at the sight of the young man who walks beside her. They are clutching hands. Surely it can't be her new boyfriend. Not another one. She goes through them faster than the rate I use tissues. Focusing on him I mentally execute a quick assessment. Much taller than her, possibly six foot three or four. The long black coat flaps open as he walks and it reaches the floor. It appears to be a thick overcoat, but it can't be as it is early autumn and the weather is mild. The straggly, unkempt hair and large round dark sunglasses along with the heavy metal tee-shirt creates a worrying impression. Abigail tucks her arm into his, then on tip-toe kisses him on the cheek. If this is her latest, I must have words with my daughter.

Suddenly I jolt back to reality. She will want to bring him onto the boat. Rufus is not partial to normal people arriving. What he will think of Abigail's new item, I shudder to imagine. There is no time to persuade Rufus to the bow where he could lay in the sunshine in peace and quiet.

In an attempt to avert any difficulty with Rufus, I jump from the stern to the towpath. 'Hi, darling. Lovely to see you.' We throw our arms around each other and hug.

Turning, I raise my head to examine the pale faced figure. The black sunglasses peer down on me. There is a half-smile, but he gives the impression of an undertaker sizing me up or a haunting figure from the Transylvanian Mountains about to lure me back to his lair. Shuddering, I try to force a welcoming expression on to my face but have no idea whether it is successful. I do not need him coming into my life looking like a sinister apparition, as I have too much to think about with the death threat hanging over me.

'This is Ryan.'

'Great. Lovely to meet you. Come on to the boat. Abigail, show Ryan the other local boats while I move Rufus to the bow.'

Abigail smiles at her boyfriend, 'Rufus is the guard dog for the boat. He's okay with me but doesn't like strangers.'

He smiles, which makes me shiver, which it should not have done. 'I like dogs.'

He will not like Rufus, or more precisely Rufus will not like him.

'I'll lead the way and persuade him to the bow where he will sit in the evening sunshine.'

Stepping on to the boat, he doesn't heed my warning but follows close behind. I expect the growl. Rufus has stirred himself from his earlier slumbers on my feet and now sits alert. I grab his collar, but he shows no aggression to the man following me. Strange.

'He's magnificent. Come here, boy.' Ryan drops on to the bench and pats his leg. Rufus ambles across to him and stands obediently in front of the stranger and allows the back of his neck to be ruffled. Unbelievable.

The conversation with Abigail's boyfriends has always been strained but I try to do my best with small talk. 'Have you dogs at home?' Immediately I regret the possible faux pas. He might have come from a broken home. Normally Abigail would brief me about a new boyfriend so that I did not embarrass myself or her, but she has never mentioned Ryan.

He laughs. Such frivolity is a surprise. I stare at the strange design on his heavy metal tee-shirt. An eerie skull is printed across the centre and crowned with the words; The End is Nigh. I shudder as I remember the death threat. Is he the Prophet of Doom? Fortunately, he is not a mind reader, and carries on in a normal voice, 'We always had dogs at home. Two, three, four or five sometimes. They came and went.'

Confusion sweeps over me; my facial expression must have given me away.

'Don't worry, Mrs Mallory. My parents are vets and as we live in a large house in the country, the dogs come and go.'

Well spoken, and animal friendly. But why does he have to look like Dracula? I imagine him kissing my daughter's neck. Shaking my head, my heart stumbles over its own rhythm as that vision will cause me several sleepless nights.

06

The choice of my clothes for the party is obvious as I peer into the cupboard that acts as my wardrobe. With a warm and overcast evening expected, my new blue hooped knitted cotton top would match with my favourite dark blue Bermuda shorts. If the temperature dips, as it can do alarmingly even on a sultry night by the water, I can nip back and select a fleece as the party is on the next boat.

Toby's message about the death threat is alarming and keeps entering my thoughts uninvited but I have attempted to pacify my anxiety by ringing journalistic colleagues. It has worked, a little, as they have assured me that nutters on the open website are common. The police do not have the manpower to trace everyone through complex technical sources. They all wished me well for the party and told me not to worry.

I have fed Rufus and he is now sprawled on the bow deck dozing. He might stir if he hears a dog on a passing boat, but he will only stand up and bark so I can leave him for the evening.

Ready for a party in which I have no interest since Toby's pronouncement, I try to put on a bright face as I pass through the boat and step up from the stern deck onto solid ground. Letitia and Russell are approaching along the path. Letitia is an outdated hippie by her appearance and only resides on *Kingfisher* infrequently. It is the most amazing ornate narrow boat, traditionally painted with brightly coloured flowers and is the most elaborate one in our little community. Tonight, Letitia is wearing a smart and expensive ensemble of matching cardigan, blouse and trousers of elaborately embroidered silks.

Wow. What an outfit. Russell and I have never met before, he always seems to be away on business. About ten years older than Letitia at sixty he is smart in a non-descript way. Letitia informed me in one of our brief conversations that he travels the world building dams.

Although I have lived here for two years, we only vaguely know each other, as they don't socialise with the other boat owners, so it's a surprise that they're here this evening. I greet them by shaking hands and make an instant judgement that I do not like Russell. He held on to my hand too long. His hand was sweaty, he reeked of aftershave and his eyes never left my breasts although I am showing no cleavage. I have classified him as a lecher.

Slipping to the other side of Letitia, I wave my hand to Jasmine who is waiting to greet us. Her party crop top has fine blue hoops, similar to mine, while her dark blue skirt is shorter than the ones I complain about Abigail wearing. If she bends over too far, we will all be able to ogle her knickers. I chuckle at the image which flashes through my mind. How Jasmine contrives to dance in that will be a revelation, but she is a party animal and I suspect she will perform many energetic dance routines later. From previous parties I recollect that she enjoys a lot of arm waving and hip thrusting when she dances.

Jasmine bubbles with excitement and sweeps her arm around to indicate the party lights and the barbecue repositioned on the far side of the towpath, which emanates onion and beefburger smells to which my stomach objects. I dislike barbecued food; burnt on the outside and undercooked in the middle. The music is already blaring out from the sound system placed on the roof of the boat while chatter and laughter from groups dotted around the area reach me. Everyone is in a party mood except me.

My husband is an embarrassment, as he sprawls on the stern seating of *Carpe Diem*, swigging from his can of strong lager. His clothes are poor workday clothes, not that he ever does much of that, and he has not shaved so that the stubble of a few days is blatantly obvious. Does he imagine that it looks like designer stubble? If so, he needs to check in a mirror as it is an untidy mess.

Benjamin, Jasmine's partner, manages a little enthusiasm as he stands to greet me, 'Welcome. Come aboard. Beer and drinks are in the galley and the action is in the bow lounge. Go through.' With that he slumps down next to Jason and picks up another beer can. Peas in a pod spring to mind, but Jonathon is rich and a bestselling author, whereas Jason is poor and a crap freelance writer.

I let Russell and Letitia go to the galley in front of me as I want to avoid being near him. He gives me the creeps. Posh voices reach me, the occupants of the *Green World* boat have arrived, which I could tell before I look around. Montgomery and Samantha are eco-activists who work in the City of London for a major tea importer but are boring to speak with. They are full of their own importance and their sole topic of conversation centres around conservation and other green issues. Of course, their narrow boat is painted green and is equipped with solar panels. Samantha grows a range of herbs on their boat which gives it a lush, interesting appearance. In my mind I refer to them as the green couple.

Waiting for them to embark, I will say hello and try to avoid them for the rest of the evening as their patronising view of the people on the canal boats annoys me. About a month ago my dislike of them erupted, mainly due to the gin that I had consumed that day at a journalist's bash, and we had a blazing argument. They were adamant that the boat owners were not a well-educated bunch and that standards were falling. During our disagreement they hinted it was possible they might move to a different location. Pompous and self-opinionated is my view of that couple.

Abigail and Ryan, strange man, have disappeared but I suspect to tank themselves up at a local pub before re-joining the party. It would be lovely to accompany them, but with a silent sigh I make my way to the galley after it has been vacated by Russell and search out a bottle of gin.

Day Two

07

My head throbs but Rufus has woken me; his wet nose nudges my arm. I glance at the bedside clock; six o'clock in the morning. The party last night had not finished until the early hours, so I haven't had that much sleep. My night had been restless with traumatic gin induced nightmares, which had woken me trembling and disorientated. He is not evil, but Ryan had loomed over me as a necropolis angel and the party revellers had become sinister and had threatened my life. Climbing from bed, my eyes are heavy and unfocussed, while my head is pounding out a relentless painful rhythm. I groan theatrically as I scrabble in the cupboard for some clothes. I dress in anything I can locate that will be suitable for a walk along the canal in the early morning. Rufus is excited and impatient. Passing up the stern steps, he waits on the towpath dancing around in energetic circles.

The gin had been good as it had given me a false sense of contentment, but the party had been crap. Although many were strangers, they were in partnerships so did not want to talk to a woman whose husband had steadily declined into a stupor on the stern deck. Wanting to avoid Russell, because of his leching and Montgomery and Samantha as a party was not a place to discuss the amount of excrement in the canal, I had chosen the gin bottle. In retrospect it had not been a sensible choice. A few gins would have been fine but I'd continually knocked back the alcohol for the duration of the party. I now regret the excesses of my evening.

Stepping up on to the towpath I groan as Rufus bounces back onto the boat to retrieve his ball from under the stern deck cushions. How can he expect anyone to play ball with him at six o'clock in the morning after going to bed at two? Most of the time he is content to walk on or off the lead, but some aspect of his psyche decides occasionally he wants to play. But why after a party?

Too dopey and confused about the day and time, I allow him to lead me along the canal through the early morning mist which swirls across the surface of the water. In excitement he rushes around sniffing at the things which interest him and leads me towards Regents' Park, preferring the wide-open spaces for a ball chase.

The death threat keeps coming back. What type of person can threaten to kill another human being? My mind is addled at the thought. The headache, the damp chill of the morning mist and not enough sleep do little to clear my mind for rational thought.

Rufus is in an energetic mood this morning and my arm aches from throwing the balls for him to chase. Much to my relief he finally decides he has had enough, and bounces towards the path which will lead us back to the canal. It is always slow as he discovers so many things to investigate in the bushes and long grass. Crossing the bridge and re-joining the empty towpath, it is too early for the keen joggers which he likes to chase, so I do not clip on his lead.

The ghostly appearance of the overhanging trees in the mist make me shiver. I have never thought of them as being overpowering before. The silence bears down on me. Anybody might be hiding waiting for their opportunity. My heart hammers as my eyes scan the area.

I quicken my pace because the swirling mist under the trees is becoming thicker. Perhaps danger is only in my imagination. Rufus bounds ahead but he keeps checking I am following. He's such a lovely dog.

It's a relief when the dark blue hull of *Serendipity* comes into view. He wanders past our boat in his usual accustomed manner. When I step on to the stern, he will join me. I want him to follow his usual routine and return to the bow, so I can sneak back into bed for a few hours' sleep, but he will not come. His behaviour is unusual. He sits on the canal side, ignoring me and staring at the water.

'Rufus, come on, let's sleep.'

Unusually he doesn't respond but sits immobile on the edge of the towpath peering into the water on the other side of Benjamin and Jasmine's boat, with his ears pricked and alert. My head throbs and I need to lie down and close my eyes. I give up calling him. He will return to the boat in his own time. I disappear down the stern steps expecting him to follow but as I reach the bottom step, he barks.

Bloody hell, you are a nuisance, Rufus. Why have you chosen this morning to be so obstinate? His continuous barking gives me no option but to return to the bank and persuade him to come back to *Serendipity*.

Strange, but his barking stops as soon as I step from the boat. He is still staring into the water. Obedient to some extent as he is no longer making a noise so I approach him hoping to encourage him to move. Patting him, I give a gentle pull on his collar, but he resolutely refuses to budge and with his size and strength I have no chance of shifting him from his position on the tow path. I let out a loud yawn and then groan loudly at this obstinate dog. I roll my eyes at him with tiredness as I am desperate to return to bed.

Peering into the canal he focuses on debris that has settled against the side, which is a common occurrence when the canal is busy with traffic and swishes the rubbish into the still water near the bank.

Rufus won't move. Why? I don't know. He stares at the debris. What has caught his attention? I stand beside him and with bleary eyes study the water. The debris is blue. Why is it familiar? I shake my head with tiredness as my gin addled brain refuses to cooperate.

A passing boat ripples the water which disturbs the debris. A hand and arm come to the surface. Is it real or did I imagine it? Glancing another boat approaches, a larger one. The water ripples more. My god, it is real. The hooped blue top and blue skirt float to the surface accompanied by an arm and leg. I am too scared to scream but a chill of fear surges through me. My eyes dart along the tow path. It is empty.

There is no one around.

Tearing my eyes away from the dead body, I degenerate into a childish whimper as I grab my phone from my jacket and dial 999. I stagger across to a tow path bench and slump down as my legs give way. Twisting around I retch into the undergrowth. Rufus sits next to my legs. I have told 999 control the quickest way to reach me though my voice had a wild note of hysteria. Did they manage to understand my frantic gabbling?

A cold shivering wind blows on the back of my neck like the touch of icy fingers. Suddenly the whole world is grey and full of menacing shadows. I lick my dry lips and wait as the silence surrounds me.

08

Certain of my sighting, the incident has removed the last of the gin from my brain. My mind is alert. The first colour had been her skirt and the second her hooped blue top. My god! Jasmine had fallen into the water, and no one had noticed.

Despite my whimpering and Rufus's barking it has brought no movement from the three nearby boats. It is better that way. I haven't the courage to rouse Benjamin and tell him his Jasmine is dead in the water. Shaking my Jason into life will not help. He is useless in a crisis, and after the drink he consumed at the party he will not know what day it is.

Gulping and worrying whether I will throw up again, my fingers reach out and I nuzzle my hand in Rufus's fur around his neck. His presence comforts me. He leans in and rests his body against my leg. Usually he would lay, but not today. His face is alert.

The siren comes closer. I wait. My hand trembles as I clutch my phone as a comfort blanket. Two young policemen come down the narrow footpath ignoring the overgrown nettles. They don't look old enough to cope with such a serious incident.

'Mrs Mallory?'

'Yes.'

'Can you...' His voice drifts away. 'Big dog.'

I clip on his lead although he does not need it as he will not leave my side. He intends to protect me. His presence is so reassuring.

'Can you...'

'There. Blue.' I stutter the words in a suffocating whisper as I point a wavering finger towards the spot.

His colleague joins him as they peer into the canal. 'Blue.'

My stomach wants to revolt again, but it would be embarrassing so I gulp in a few deep breaths of air. Whether it will do the trick I can't be sure. No passing boats ripple the water. Will they be able to catch sight of the body?

His colleague stands on the tow path peering but doesn't bend down, 'Do you need a hook?'

'No, I can reach.'

He lays on the ground and stretches his hand down, 'Got it.'

My eyes follow their movements and their conversation reaches me. Holding my breath in anticipation, I hope that it will just be a piece of debris and the officers will laugh at me. Then I shall return to the boat and sleep.

'The lady is right; it is a body.'

I sit frozen with terror. Jasmine. How has this happened? She was so alive and vibrant at the party. When had she fallen overboard? Why hadn't anyone noticed? Was she too drunk to swim and save herself? Why didn't she scream? All these questions and many more whizz through my brain at the speed of lightning while I remain motionless and silent.

'I'll call the centre.' He drifts along the path speaking into his radio.

The officer who had lain on the path stands and while keeping a careful eye on Rufus sits next to me. His arriving half smile has gone, and he has a deep serious expression.

'Where do you live?'

'There, on *Serendipity*.'

'Who else lives there?'

That is a tricky question. Is he just referring to last night?

Although my mind is addled as the colours in the water indicated without doubt that it is Jasmine, I will go for a non-committal approach.

'My husband, Jason, and sometimes my daughter Abigail.'

He frowns and his brow furrows in confusion, 'Why sometimes?'

'She lives in Paddington as she is at Uni so comes home at any time.'

'Did she last night?'

The shock of the discovery has dissipated. Despite the gin, I have come to the realisation of the terrible day.

'Constable, you need to know that last night there was a party on *Carpe Diem*. All the residents of the other boats attended as far as I can remember.' I open my arm to indicate the swathe of other boats along the bank.

'Thank you.' But his frown indicates that he is not impressed.

'From the colour of the clothing, do you have any idea who it might be.'

'Yes.' He raises his eyebrows. 'Jasmine from *Carpe Diem* was wearing a dark blue skirt and a blue hooped top at the party last night.'

09

After the discovery, the call from the constable produces a flood of activity. Police appear from nowhere. By then several of the nearby boat residents have risen and look out bleary eyed from their boats which are tightly packed along the canal side. It is strange but no one ventures out to discover why the area is crawling with police. Perhaps they consider it to be no concern of theirs. It strikes me as uncharitable.

My stomach is in a state of turmoil and I want neither food nor drink. My mouth is dry, my muscles stiff and I want somewhere to hide where I can close my eyes and sleep. When I wake up it will all have been a nightmare. Weakness overwhelms me and I collapse back onto the stern seats which is our usual place for sitting in the milder weather.

Wherever Rufus has been I have no idea, but he comes from somewhere inside the boat and sits next to me watching the activities. It is the wrong place to sit. The last view I need is of the police and others focusing on the water. The vision of her floating body haunts me. When will they pull poor Jasmine out?

The thought terrifies me. As I stand up intending to move and reposition myself inside the boat where I will be unable to view the proceedings, two policemen approach along the tow path. Rufus stands. He has been content to watch the operations taking place nearby, but the police have stopped at the step to the stern. Rufus is an intelligent dog.

The police officers chat but I cannot hear their words. One goes to step down. Rufus lifts his head and howls but settles to a growl as I gently touch him on his head. The second policeman laughs. Not appropriate for the morning but during my journalistic days on news reports I have realised that the emergency services have a graveyard humour. It is despicable to me but, there again, for all the money on earth I could not do their job.

The officer who had laughed faces me with a serious expression. 'Mrs Mallory, is it alright for me to come aboard?'

I hesitate, 'Wait a minute and I will tie Rufus up, and then you can step down.'

I focus on the officer in his thirties, who doesn't wait for me to secure Rufus but climbs aboard. Rufus howls and barks making it quite clear that he wants no intruders on the boat. A small smile touches my lips as he is trying to protect me, although his noise even makes me fearful. I grab his collar, but I am likely to lose the battle as he is stronger than me.

The officer continues to smile. He raises the flat of his hand. 'Steady fella. Settle.'

Rufus stops moving and barking but growls deep and low.

'Let go of his collar.'

Is the man mad after such a display of aggression? He focuses intently on Rufus. Opening the flat of his hand, Rufus sits and growls, although it doesn't sound as menacing as previously.

Despite the trauma that rifles through my body, I am impressed at the way this stranger has approached the tricky situation. I had expected Rufus to be aggressive and move towards the policeman baring his teeth. The officer moves his finger across his chest and Rufus quietens and lays down. It is unbelievable. I am in total awe of this stranger.

The officer points to the opposite seat. I nod, 'Please do.'

He is a huge man and occupies almost two seats.

Stuttering as it is the best I can do. 'Can we move away from the activity?'

'Don't worry if that is your concern. No significant progress will happen for hours and by then the tents and personnel will be in place and you will be asked to leave the vicinity.'

'Oh.'

'I am sure you have watched plenty of television detective programmes. We need to establish who was at last night's party and their current location.' The smooth way he moves from the mundane to the critical worries me. Not that it should. He is only doing his job.

'You were at the party?'

I nod, 'All the time, I was one of the last to leave.'

My stomach grips at the anticipation of the follow up questions.

'Thanks.' He scribes the details in his notebook. 'These are pure formalities at this stage. People drunk at parties on canal boats can often lead to a precarious situation. The outcome can be obvious. Who else from your family is on the boat now?'

Shock ravages through my body at the simple question. I didn't know. Because of the decline in our marriage recently Jason had opted, normally in a drunken stupor, to sleep on the single beds in the lounge. The other cabin is Abigail's but whether she had turned up with Ryan, I had no idea.

I felt a compulsion to explain my lack of a quick answer. He waits. 'Jason my husband has a drinking partner, Benjamin from *Carpe Diem*.' My voice becomes shrill, but I can do nothing to settle it. 'They often crash out in their lounge when they have had too much to drink.'

He rubs his nose in a thoughtful fashion as he watches me.

'My daughter Abigail and her boyfriend, Ryan, might have stayed.' I shudder as I mention his name. I am gabbling but it is impossible to slow down and speak in a more reasoned manner, I flap my hand in a flippant gesture. 'They are at Uni and have digs at Paddington but move between here and there.' It is an exaggeration as I had never met Ryan before last night. Perhaps I should not have said it. But to try to correct it will put me in an uneasy position. I am not handling this well.

While his face has a friendly expression, I fear his next question.

'Mrs Mallory. If you are unsure who is aboard, shall we check?'

This is too much. What an embarrassment. We walk the length of the boat, but it is empty. Not to know who is on board is one issue but the serious matter is where are my husband and daughter?

10

After the police officer has left, I ring Jason and Abigail but receive no reply. Checking my watch as the sunshine breaks through the clouds it is only ten o'clock. Time is dragging this morning. It seems a lifetime ago since Rufus woke me demanding his walk. I scrub a hand across my face trying to remove the tiredness. I no longer want to return to bed as if I close my eyes, the image of Jasmine's dead body floating amongst the debris will appear. I shudder.

Normally, after a party, I would not encounter either Jason or Abigail until noon. From experience both will have been slaughtered by too much alcohol and the day after the party will be treated with calm and perhaps a hair of the dog in the evening but nothing else.

Sometimes I try to remember back a few years when I did not have Rufus. I would have joined Jason and Abigail in the dreamy lands of a hangover by staying in bed until lunchtime, but that is an indulgence from the past. Rufus will not permit such slovenly behaviour.

Given the circumstances my mind is relaxed about Jason and Abigail not being here. Strangely I hold no fears over their safety. But my mind is in a whirl. Jasmine. She had been so alive yesterday. But today she is down in the murky waters of the canal until the police machine remove her. As the relationship with Jasmine comes to me, it makes me think.

Many people meeting her, even in the middle of the day, assume she is tipsy. But I cannot remember her drinking substantial amounts. Last night at the party, we hardly spoke, no doubt due to the repercussions from the barbecue argument.

Shivering, I cannot dwell on her, or the death threat I received yesterday, which suddenly rears into my mind. Nothing else for it but to distract myself from thinking. Housework. I chuckle. Should it be called boatwork? That is ridiculous. Housework will do. Rufus sleeps soundly, which suits me, as I can hoover, dust and polish. I will start at the bow.

Reaching the stern deck, I stand for a moment enjoying the fresh air. The blue and white police tapes festoon the length of the towpath. A solitary figure comes into view which brings a smile from me. He hobbles with a left sided limp. Matey, his black labrador, limps alongside of him. His dog is never on a lead. These realisations come to me suddenly. What did Jasmine drink? Why was Matey never on a lead? My head needs no more turmoil as it is already awash with unanswered questions.

I wave enthusiastically. 'Hi, dad.'

He smiles and waves but pauses looking around at the police activities. Moving to the rear of the stern deck I offer him a hand down the deep step which he accepts with a smile. Matey turns on the towpath and spreadeagles at the entrance to the boat. He and Rufus are fine together when I go for walks with him and dad, but he will never come on board. An unwritten rule of dogs? I boggle at the thought.

'Tea in the dining area?'

'That will be perfect, Amanda.'

He has never wanted great hugs of welcome. After giving me the usual kiss on the cheek, I wander away to make the tea.

We slide in either side of the fixed dining table. As I move opposite him, I am not happy about his appearance. The anorak which he hasn't removed reminds me of walks with him in the past. It must be thirty years old. The grey cardigan he is wearing underneath has dubious food remains down the front and is buttoned incorrectly.

'Dad, your cardigan looks squiffy. What's wrong with it.' I will allow him the chance to adjust it.

Looking down, 'Not buttoned correctly and a variety of breakfasts down it.'

Smiling and wanting to help, 'I can wash and iron anything for you, I've told you many times.'

Taking his sip of tea, he ignores my words, 'The police

have cordoned off the area and are allowing no one in or out.'

'Did they allow you through as you have relatives on one of the boats?'

'No, the Sergeant who arrived recognised me. We worked together on some of my cases when he was a constable. He radioed ahead. He is a good copper and if he is on the case, we should get a result.'

Gulping my hot tea, his words gradually filter into my addled brain. 'Case? What case? It's obvious, Jasmine fell into the canal when she was drunk.'

He studies his mug of tea with a quizzical expression. 'Possibly, but one of the first constables on the scene spotted something to investigate.'

Panic grips me and I lean forward. 'What! What! Don't do this to me dad. What had he spotted? I made the discovery and reported it to the police.'

Dad grins. 'Good girl. That was the right action. I do not know what has caused the suspicion, but they will follow it through and decide whether it is relevant or not.'

He must have noticed the expression on my face. 'Don't worry you have done nothing wrong.'

'You came to the party, didn't you dad?'

He nods in an absentminded manner and appears thoughtful. Perhaps, with his background he will offer an insight into the police activities. 'The invite had been given to me so I popped in as I walked Matey.'

On recollection, all my friends give him invites, though he rarely attends. So why did he come to last night's party?

'Any reason for attending?'

'Yes, I like Benjamin's books. Exactly the political thrillers that I enjoy. I had a couple of beers with him and we had a good chat, and I said hello to Jasmine.' Dad grins with satisfaction. 'He promised to give me a copy of the latest one before it is published.'

While I want to talk to him about his reading, the police on the towpath demand my attention. 'Dad, if we are sectioned off, what happens next?'

He peers around in a distracted manner. At that point Rufus wanders into the dining area and recognises him. He sits next to dad and receives the expected tickle of his fur on the back of his neck. 'I assume that a copper came to ask about the residents and your details but not much else.'

He still appears distracted as though he has something on his mind. 'Yes.' I watch him closely. I am worried about him. Shall I tell him about the death threat I received? No. I'll leave it a few days as I don't want to worry him.

After several slurps of tea, 'There will be formal interviews about the party and events last night. We sometimes conduct them in homes but the canal boats will be too difficult for confidentiality so I expect there will be a police caravan.' He looks up at me from his attention on Rufus, 'Just tell them what you saw and what you did. Don't hold back to protect people or yourself. Being open and honest is the quickest way to reach a result.'

11

After dad has left, I intend to resume my domestic duties. Before I have a chance to restart a Police Community Officer appears on the towpath. 'Is now a convenient time to take your formal statement about last night's party and this morning's events?'

It's a surprise that a Community Officer is asking me, as I thought it would be a policeman who conducted the questioning. I nod my acceptance. He doesn't step on to the boat, which confuses me. Are we going to have the interview on the towpath? 'If you will come with me.' It then registers that the questioning will happen at another location. My stomach twists and with the remnants of too much gin still lurking in my system, I am distinctly queasy.

Grabbing my jumper, I step on to the towpath. Although it is mid-morning the amount of police activity has increased. Men and women in white coveralls with their hair covered and wearing face masks step on to *Carpe Diem*. Benjamin is nowhere to be seen. I have not spotted him this morning.

An elaborate tented structure that reaches the water has been constructed over the towpath. Several police and forensic guys are in small motorboats and firefighters are now securing the scaffolding that holds the tent. I gulp. Poor Jasmine is in there, not that she will know anything about the activities. It is too horrendous to contemplate and I avert my gaze. Life is difficult and unpredictable. Jasmine was full of life and energy yesterday and now she has gone.

The gentle breeze cools my hot flushed cheeks as I obediently follow the young man. The early morning mist has vanished and the sun shines from a perfect blue sky. The knot in my stomach twists as I dread what will happen at the interview. Trying to reason with myself that I have done nothing wrong, doesn't work. Will both my nerve and stomach hold out for an interrogation?

Following the Community Officer, who sets off at a cracking pace, we climb the footpath on the bank. When we reach the top and the cul-de-sac of residential houses the small road is full of police cars. My attention goes to the black van near to where we have joined the road. The signage is small, but as I pass it, the gold lettering, Coroner, glistens in the sunlight. My mind spirals out of control, stuck on thoughts of Jasmine's lifeless body floating in the canal. Tears fill my eyes and I avert my gaze and study the grey boring footpath and the equally boring houses alongside.

We are heading to a large black caravan labelled police. The young man offers me a hand up the three steep steps. How old does he think I look? With a grimace I decline his offer of help. He approaches the first door on the right of the grey plastic walled interior and ushers me inside, 'Take a seat, someone will be with you shortly.'

I move my head slowly up and down, as the ability to form words is an impossible task. Despite wearing a jumper too thick for the morning's sunny weather, I shiver. The stark grey room with a matching desk and three hard plastic chairs of different colours, resembles a desolate cell from a nightmare.

The door of the cell bursts open and a man in sweatshirt and jeans bounds in, and flicks the door shut with a swift kick of his foot. It doesn't close but bounces back at him. He responds by kicking it, a little more viciously, a second time. Thankfully this time it shuts with a sharp click. How many more times would he have kicked it before accepting defeat and closing it in the normal manner? The corners of his mouth twitch in amusement, 'This caravan is falling to bits.'

Not helped by you kicking it comes to mind, but I make no comments. With a thwack he drops a folder and a note book on to the table. Is his boisterous and noisy arrival deliberately intended to unnerve witnesses. If so, it is working. I'm trembling and my clenched hands rest in my lap.

Sensing he has finally settled in his seat as the noise has quietened, I push my blonde hair away from my face and study him. About thirty, fat faced with stubble and dishevelled hair, he does not endear himself to me.

He rests his elbows on the table and smirks with self-assurance, 'Okay to call you, Amanda?'

Nodding, is all I can manage as I'm still struggling to articulate words.

'I am Detective Constable Martin Smith. Do you know why you are here?'

My hackles rise. I am not in a tolerant mood and we will not make progress until he stops asking bloody daft questions.

I lick my dry lips and force both my mind and mouth to cooperate, so that I can form some sensible words. 'Because I called the police this morning.'

'No. Let me explain. Your statement this morning to the first officers was clear and succinct. What job do you do?'

'Journalist.'

'Ah, that accounts for the precision. No questions about that for the moment but we might come back to you later, although I am not dealing with that aspect of the investigation. I want to talk to you about last night's party.'

I gulp and need three attempts at forming the single word, before I manage to mutter, 'Okay.'

'Did you meet Jasmine at the party?'

'Briefly.' My stomach concerns me as it wants to trip out as it is rattling and rolling in an ominous fashion.

'When is the last time you saw her?'

Tricky question. I mull over my response. 'I think it was about ten o'clock, but I cannot be sure.'

'Where did the meeting take place?'

From the laid-back attitude when he had first arrived, he has changed to intense quick-fire questions as he leans forward, with his eyes firmly fixed on my face.

'It must have been in the galley.'

'Are you certain?'

'Yes, I never left the galley all the time I was at the party.' But I had only a vague feeling about the latter part of the evening although I didn't intend to divulge that snippet of information.

'May I presume that is where the party drinks were?' His mouth tilts up to one side and he smirks with amusement. Irritating man.

'Yes.' But I cannot look at him any longer and transfer my focus to the notebook in his hand. He is silent. Is he waiting for me to look up? I have no option but to comply. The smirk has vanished to be replaced with a deadpan expression that I expect of the police.

'How long have you known her?'

'About two years since we moved into the boat next to theirs.'

'Were you on friendly terms?'

'Yes.' I agonise whether to explain about the tiff we had yesterday before the party about the positioning of the barbecue. I decide against it and attempt to convince myself it is not important.

'Have you just thought of something that is relevant to my questions?'

I panic internally and my stomach lets out a terrifying grumble. Is he a mind reader as well as a policeman? With great effort I concentrate on keeping my facial expression neutral but am unsure whether I have achieved this aim. 'No, I was thinking about poor Jasmine.'

His brown eyes squint suspiciously as he stares at me. He does not believe me. My neutral expression was unsuccessful, but I will not jeopardise myself further so opt to stay silent.

12

Ambling back to the boat, the interview with the police was not a total disaster although it could have been better. My answers had been short and succinct and I hadn't elaborated or offered any additional information. I hope there are no future questions about what happened at the party. The thought gives me the shivers as I retrace my steps down the footpath towards the towpath.

A nagging thought enters my mind. Had I really been that drunk that I could not remember what happened at the party? Perhaps the death threat had upset me and I didn't want to participate so I stayed in the galley all the evening. But who did I talk to and about what?

Hopefully I had insignificant conversations as people drifted into the galley for drinks. My mind must have been elsewhere. It is a worrying thought.

Right. Try to be positive. While I wait for Jason to appear I'll resume the domestic duties and finish tidying and cleaning the boat. Earlier I left a message, but he has not returned my call. Approaching the boat, the mystery is solved as Jason lounges in a relaxed manner on the stern deck seating, as though he has not a care in the world.

'Hi.' Stepping down on the deck, in my usual manner, I kiss him on the cheek, but it draws little response from him. 'Where have you been? It's late morning.'

He scratches at his stubble which appears even scruffier this morning. He's a total slob these days. 'I crashed in Benjamin's lounge last night. It was late and I didn't want to disturb you.'

'Thanks, that's thoughtful.' I want to mend a few bridges with him as we have bickered a lot recently. I could do with a bit of moral support as discovering Jasmine in the water this morning won't leave me.

I wait for him to continue and focus on his face. He shifts his body a few times and looks down at the deck. He must be suffering from a hangover just like me. His face is tight and pinched.

With a hesitant cough, he lifts his head, 'As usual, we drank too much so I was still asleep when the police arrived and woke us. They asked a few questions and as they wanted to examine the boat we were driven to the police station to fill in the details of last night.'

'Why didn't they interview you in the caravan?'

'What caravan?'

'In the cul-de-sac at the end of the footpath. That's where they asked me questions.'

Rubbing his forehead, 'I assume that the caravan arrived later. It was early when the police wanted to talk to us. They told us they had found a body in the water. It was only after we reached the police station that they informed me, and I presume Benjamin, that it was Jasmine.

'I found her.'

His head jolts up and his hands tremble as he grips the side of the seat. Wide eyed he stares at me. 'On a walk with Rufus?'

I blink in agreement and manage to fractionally bob my head which is not easy. Words have left me again as the shock of the find returns. The images swarm through my mind.

'You poor thing.' Standing, he crosses to where I sit, places his arm around me and kisses me on top of my head. 'It must have come as a shock.' He flops back into his seat and yawns in an exaggerated manner. 'Are you okay?'

'Yes, the initial shock passed quickly but the image of her floating in the canal keeps coming back to me.'

'Yes, it must do.'

Shuffling around he repositions himself on the seat and reverts back to his half vacant abstracted expression. He rubs his hands together although the weather is not cold. After a couple of hesitations which is not like him, he lets out a long groan, 'I was the last person to see her.'

'How do you know? Did the police tell you?'

'No, I worked it out for myself.'

'It was near the end of the party and people were beginning to drift away.'

'Had I gone by then?'

'No, I don't think so.'

Jason is having the same problem as me in trying to remember the details of what has happened through an alcohol laden mind. I wait for him to explain. After rapidly blinking his eyes, he gives an anxious little cough, 'Jasmine asked me to give her a hand with the barbecue. People had been eating late and it was still alight, but she wanted it extinguished as she didn't want it burning all night. Because it was so hot it took time and by then there were only a few people left.'

He puts his head on one side.

'What?'

'It was a surprise to observe you eating a burger last night. I didn't think you liked them.'

Shaking my head, 'You must have had too much to drink. I didn't have one.'

He rubs his eyes, and stifles another yawn, 'It was only from a distance, but I saw you ladling on the tomato sauce.'

Shaking my head. 'Not me.'

A police officer appears on the towpath. 'Can we have another word with you please, Mr Mallory.'

Jason groans. 'Yes. Do I have to accompany you to the police station again?'

'No, that will not be necessary as the caravan is in place, the detective is there waiting for you.'

'Okay.' He kisses me on my head again. 'This has all been too much for me. I will visit mum and might stay over if that's alright with you.'

It isn't. Because I want moral support, but whether Jason can provide it with the mood he has adopted in recent months is seriously in doubt. I keep my irritated thoughts to myself. 'Okay, let me know what you decide.'

'You'll be alright here on your own as you have Rufus.'

The dog is not going to give me moral support. He has no sympathy for how I must be feeling.

Jason steps up to the towpath and walks away chatting

to the police officer.

Wanting to keep my mind occupied so that it doesn't dwell on the events and the questioning I will continue with domestic duties. As Jason has come back and changed, I would do the washing. Picking up the blue and white top I wore last night, it is stained down the front. I assume that I had spilt my drink. I study the stain. Grease and tomato sauce. My legs weaken and I clutch the side for support. I denied eating a burger. What else happened that I cannot remember?

13

Domestic duties are wearing thin, they have not distracted me and my mind is still in turmoil. I must speak with people. The subject doesn't matter. The loneliness is adding to my problems as the terrible images invade my mind. My phone bleeps. Reaching over I flick it open, *Be over to see you later mum.* I smile to no one, at least Abigail will talk to me. Most of the time it's hard to stop her chattering on about her life, but today it is just what I need.

Glancing through the round side window, Benjamin steps down on to his boat. If the police let me, I will speak with him. It will be difficult, but I have lived next to him and Jasmine for two years, so I consider it a duty to offer my condolences.

A policeman stands on the path. 'Can I visit Benjamin?'

He sizes me up and down, 'Yes, Mrs Mallory.'

The use of my name sends a shiver through me, but a deep breath calms me and I proceed with my mission.

Stepping onto the stern deck of *Carpe Diem,* I peer down the steps trying to catch sight of him. The smell of the leftover party hits me. Stale food and beer assault my nostrils making my over sensitive stomach roll with disgust. 'Are you there Benjamin? It's Amanda.'

'Yes. Come in. Ignore the mess and come through to the front seating area, I've opened the windows wide.'

Holding my breath, I pass the galley, dining area and bedrooms. While the front area still has a residual smell it is being quickly cleared by the cool breeze which blows across the surface of the canal. Benjamin has an expressionless face and it is hard to gauge his reaction to the devastating news. I suppose it is to be expected as he is never a great one for facial gestures. Seeing him brings tears to my eyes. I step forward, go up on tip toe and hug him. 'I'm so sorry, Benjamin, Jasmine's death must be devastating for you.'

'Yes, the morning has been horrendous.' He opens his hand for me to sit on the opposite chair to him. 'Thanks for coming, I do appreciate it.'

Words leave me apart from trite ones such as what a nice person she was, so I wrestle to find something to say. 'You will be busy, so would you like me to clean up your boat?'

'That's kind, Amanda, but let's leave it. Will you stay so we can talk?'

'Of course.'

He shakes his head, 'I'm not busy as I cannot think of anything I need to do.'

'Have you told Jasmine's relatives?'

He shrugs. 'Like me she has none. We are both from single parent families with no brothers or sisters. Both our mothers are dead.'

'I never realised.' I blurt out the words in embarrassment. Why didn't I know more about the background of the couple that had been my neighbours? Is it because I wasn't interested enough to find out, or that perhaps, they didn't want to reveal their personal history? If it is the former then I am to blame. Should I have taken more time to get to know them?

'Jason has gone over to his mother's. I can ring him if you want company.'

'No, thanks. Jason is fine and we have a few beers and talk about the football and that's it.' He glances at his watch, 'It's gone midday and it might help me settle if I can talk about Jasmine.'

'I will willingly listen and talk about her.'

In an abrupt movement he eases his tall frame from the chair and stands. Stretching his arms, he lifts his head and lets out a long slow sigh. Then relaxing, his dark eyes focus on me, 'I need a whiskey. Gin and tonic for you?'

After my gin induced memory lapses, I resolved to give up drinking alcohol, but I cannot refuse him. 'Just a small one, Benjamin.' Without another word he disappears into the galley. The sound of bottles being moved and the chink of ice rattling in a glass reach me. Returning to the seating area he carries two glasses with generous measures of alcohol.

Breathing out a drawn in breath, he sinks back down into his chair. He focuses on me, holds up his glass but does not offer the toast to Jasmine as I expected and remains silent. I raise my glass and think of Jasmine. Why doesn't he say her name?

He places his glass down on a nearby surface and stares with unnerving directness at me, 'You will not know the reason why we decided on the party.'

Perplexed a little at his abrupt introduction to our discussion, I will remain silent and listen as I expect that is what he wants.

'We had decided to split up.'

A short silence follows while I digest his words. They are unexpected. 'Benjamin this is very sudden. You seemed happy together.'

He spreads his hands in a regretful gesture and shrugs, 'We decided to leave each other. The party was a farewell to all that knew us. I've already found a flat in Camden and intended putting the boat up for sale the day after the party.'

'You don't have to tell me if you do not wish to, but why choose to split? I thought you made a good couple.'

He rubs his chin and stares with unblinking solemnity. The long look is devastating. It's as though I've completed some horrendous misdemeanour. I pick up my drink and sip, readjust my position on the seat and push a stray strand of hair behind my ear.

In no hurry to continue, he sips his whiskey and stares out the window. Two moorhens are scurrying around not far from the boat. Pursing his lips, he refocuses on me, 'We drifted together by accident when we met at the agent's office who rented and sold boats. Jasmine wanted a boat share as she did not have enough money to buy one but liked the idea of an artistic community on the canal.'

'What about you?'

'I was in a rut and while my writing is successful, I do not make friends easily and thought a canal boat would make a change. She was an attractive woman. When the agent explained she didn't have boats shares, I joked she could share with me. We went from there.'

Taking a large sip of gin. 'The story is unbelievable. None of us knew.'

'No, we told no one. But I found working on the boat noisy and cramped although I stayed with it until Jasmine started having an affair.'

I swallowed the rest of the gin.

'We were never in love, but I enjoyed the sex with her. The affair started a few months ago and I decided to act but I was being pressurised by my publisher for the next book and so I drifted for the six weeks or so since I found out. I told her last week I was selling the boat and she could stay until the exchange of contracts, but I was moving out. She took it in good heart, there was no animosity between us, and we agreed on the party.'

'Oh, I don't know what to say.'

He gives a false laugh. 'I wanted to tell someone, and you are the person on the boats that I have been most comfortable with.'

'What about Jason?'

'Nice guy to have a beer with and watch the football, and I know he is your husband, but he is a waste of space.'

I couldn't disagree with the sentiment as he only ever had short conversations with me and appeared disinterested in any gossip or news that I wanted to convey.

'I shall leave the boat as soon as the police have finished with me. Would you mind telling Montgomery and Samantha on *Green World*.' I nod in agreement. 'And Russell and Letitia. As I have never liked either couple, they are far too pretentious for me, I don't feel a personal meeting is warranted.'

Without asking he drifts to the galley and returns with the bottles of whiskey and gin.

He is expecting it to be a long session. Even if he was not in love with her, he was intimate with her for two years so he must be in shock from the accident. I will try to talk about the positive aspects of Jasmine. I mull over various approaches but I am not making any progress. In the end I blurt out, 'I got on well with Jasmine.' It is a pretty pathetic statement and a warm flush spreads across my cheeks.

Pouring the spirits, he raises his eyebrows. 'Don't feel you have to say nice things about her for my sake. She was moody and I'll say it to you, a freeloader.'

The heart to heart and the truths that are emerging are making me uncomfortable, but I will stick with him.

'But there was one strange aspect about her that perplexed me.'

Fearing to ask as I did not want more bad news, I had little chance of avoiding the issue, so I put my head on one side in a questioning gesture.

'She set up painting with her easel in different spots.'

'Yes, she had become a familiar feature locally.'

'She chatted to people passing a lot which means she completed little painting, but in the two years she never showed me a completed painting but maintained she sold them for thousands.'

I am becoming confused by this conversation. 'Why did you call her a freeloader?'

'Any money she claimed to earn from her painting was put in the bank to buy her own boat. In all the time she lived with me she never offered me rent or paid for any food or drink. When she wanted new clothes, she either asked me or took the money from my wallet but not in a deceptive way.'

This chat has been too revealing for my liking so I will return to a more general topic. 'When are the police likely to conclude the case so you can go to your new flat.'

'They have told me little except that it is being treated as a suspicious death.'

My eyes open wide. 'I assumed they were checking the circumstance for an accidental death.'

Benjamin shakes his head, 'The police maintain there are other factors but will give me no further details.'

'Didn't she fall into the water after drinking too much?'

'Amanda, Jasmine did not drink alcohol.'
I lick my dry lips and down my third gin.

14

Despite offering once again, to clean up *Carpe Diem* of the leftovers from the party, Benjamin declines and picks up his phone. I listen to his side of the conversation. He has contacted a cleaning firm to come in and bin the lot. Worried about his revelations I have asked him whether he wants to come to *Serendipity* for a meal. He thanks me for the offer but informs me his publisher is taking him out to dinner.

Drifting back to our boat I try to contemplate the information he has shared but it is too difficult to comprehend when my mind is in a mess from the party last night. The beefburger comes to mind. I never eat them and would have denied it infinitum, but the grease and tomato sauce tell a different story. It concerns me that I remember so little about the evening. Who did I chat to? Did I make a complete fool of myself?

Unable to answer these questions I step onto the boat and decide Rufus needs a walk. It won't help a great deal. Our usual pattern is to embark on a long walk when I want to think about my work. At the current time thinking is the last thing I need to do.

Another issue strikes me as I step down to the stern deck. I have not eaten for most of the day as my stomach would have rebelled. Three large gins with Benjamin has not added to a settled stomach nor to clarity of mind. It is early afternoon, and the gin will smell on my breath. Mints. There must be some on the boat. I will locate them and then persuade Rufus to move from his lengthy sleep in the sunshine on the bow.

I shake my head. Dog logic confuses me. Why does the dog want to walk and play ball at six o'clock in the morning and on a nice afternoon prefers to sleep?

Having roused him from his slumbers by calling his name, he comes for a treat of biscuits which he always receives when he responds.

Before I leave the boat, I glance outside to check on the

police activity. Dad is ambling along the tow path with Matey. I locate out of date Polo mints in the drawer, stuff three in my mouth, put the kettle on, and climb up from the boat to meet him.

Matey assumes his usual position on the towpath as I help dad down the steps. 'Kettle's on. Any reason for the visit as I saw you this morning?'

'No, Matey wanted a walk and I thought I would check on you. It is a big deal becoming involved in a suspicious death case. Before I retired, I noticed the effect it had on principal witnesses. Confident and skilled people would go to pieces even though there were no possible implications of them committing the murder.'

Nervously, I moisten my dry lips then continue crunching the polo mints. The single word, murder, reverberates through my brain. 'Do you think it's murder?' My voice is quiet and I almost whisper the words.

Dad grins. 'You haven't made the tea and have not given me a chance to explain. You are a journalist so you can appreciate the meaning. Calm down. It's a suspicious death, which can from my experience mean many things, but one outcome is most likely.'

I lean closer. 'Is the delay in reaching a conclusion significant? What outcome?'

While he is not on this case his Chief Inspector status will have given him an insight.

He laughs. 'Thanks for the tea and I'll have a biscuit from the tin even though they were not offered.'

He makes me grin despite the circumstances as he always has done all through my life. I retrieve the biscuit tin, which is full of his favourites, custard creams and chocolate digestives.

'Dad, talk to me. The police are still here.'

He selects another biscuit. A chocolate digestive this time which he dunks in his tea. Can he have lost his way in life as his cardigan is still buttoned incorrectly.

'I'll tell you the reason.' He leans forward and I do the

same as though we are conspiratorial.

'Yes.'

'The local pathologist who has been here for years is a pillock.'

'Dad, what has that got to do with the case?'

'Shall I tell you? It will be graphic.' His eyes twinkle with amusement.

'Okay. Carry on.'

Despite all the tents to keep the operations from the public, the pathologist with a suspicious death will want to examine the body in the position it was found. If someone dies in bed then that is straightforward. But in this case, it is cold, wet and thoroughly unpleasant to be surrounded by foul smelling canal water while measurements and tests take place. Believe me as I have been on the boats that are under the tent it is horrendous. They will delay until the best precautions and mechanism are in place for their security. Boats, platforms, protection from the weather. So, it takes a long time to come to the initial conclusion. It is nothing to worry about. These operations are painstakingly slow.'

'Yes, I understand.'

Should I relate the strange conversation with Benjamin? No, too complicated. 'It's been a difficult few days.'

Although the main problem with my death threat had only come yesterday, it seems a lifetime away.

He sips his tea.

I plunge in to reveal my worrying news. 'Yesterday, the newspaper editor, Toby, informed me there has been a death threat against me.'

He drops his biscuit, 'Tell me.'

'The editor and police have dismissed it as a nutter.'

'What did it say, do you know?'

Suddenly dad's eyes are focused and alert.

Do not pursue the case of the dead woman in the churchyard, otherwise the reporter will join her.'

He rubs a hand across his face.

Without any explanation he rises from the bench seat

leaving the discarded biscuit and his half-finished cup of tea. Rufus is flopped in the corridor outside of the bedroom cabins. 'Here boy.' As usual he comes immediately as he always does for dad.

Bemused by his actions, I want to comment but dad appears so determined that I remain silent.

'Lay Rufus, Good boy. I'll be back, don't leave the boat.'

'Dad, what is this all about?'

'Patience, Amanda, stay there.'

'But you haven't finished your tea.'

He steps up on the towpath where he instructs Matey to stay. A strange action as Matey goes everywhere with him. My mother-in-law comes into view, Dad waits for her to approach and speaks to her. After assisting Linda on to the boat he disappears into the mist that is once again forming over the canal.

15

It is rare for my mother-in-law to visit the boat. We get along tolerably well but have never developed a deep friendship. To be fair she never interferes in our marriage and keeps her thoughts to herself, but she dotes on her only son. I suspect that in his younger days he was thoroughly spoiled. Until recently if Jason wanted to visit his mother, we would go together to her flat in nearby Fitzrovia. In recent months he no longer asks me to accompany him. I have pondered this change of attitude but have never reached a satisfactory conclusion.

I grasp her hand to steady her down the last step and ensure her new full length blue coat does not catch on the steps. As usual her appearance is smart and her short white hair is immaculately styled. 'Hello, dear.' She kisses me on the cheek and sits on a stern deck seat without taking off her coat. I assume it is a quick visit but why has she come?

A long pause follows while she settles herself but all the while her eyes survey me with a strange unreadable expression. 'Jason does not know I've come to visit you.'

Even more mysterious.

'He has gone out to meet friends to watch the football this evening.' This news does not come as a surprise as he normally goes to the next boat and watches with Benjamin, but he will be unavailable as he is going out for the evening with his publisher.

Linda is not a woman to beat about the bush. She is often succinct and direct even if it offends. She gives me a wary look as she focuses on my face. 'Have you noticed a change in Jason's behaviour over the last couple of months?'

Normally she avoids talking about her son to me. There is no point in being coy and defensive as I have been seriously considering ending the relationship despite twenty years of marriage. 'Yes. He is more moody, insular and often snaps at me for no good reason.'

'It's not a criticism of you, my dear,' she leans across and gives my arm a reassuring pat, 'but have you provoked him, as I know you have a short temper.'

I bite my tongue at the instant response which rises in my throat. Just because my marriage is disintegrating there is no point in taking it out on Linda. 'No, I have not lost my temper with him as he tends to avoid talking to me unless he wants money.'

Linda frowns but I must tell the truth about him. She presses her mouth into a tight line.

Undeterred, I will be brave although it might incur her wrath. 'Have you found him any different recently?'

'Yes, my dear, that is why I came to talk with you. Do you think he is ill and is keeping it from us?'

That is not an idea that occurred to me, because he is never ill. I shake my head.

'I agree with you his appearance is no different to normal.'

That at least is positive as Linda will use her skills, developed when she was a nurse to identify attributes that I might not have noticed.

'Did he tell you about Jasmine?'

'Yes. Fell into the water and drowned during a party. Tragic but it happens when people drink too much.'

'It's mysterious, because she did not drink alcohol.'

Her eyes flick towards the towpath, 'Here comes your dad with someone else. I'll let you chat with them in peace. Let me know if you get an insight into his change of behaviour.'

She gives me a brush of my cheek with her lips and steps up to the towpath, gives a cheery wave towards dad and strides away. My stomach turns, as dad is accompanied by the policeman who interviewed me this morning. I pop another mint into my mouth but assume the alcohol on my breath is no longer noticeable.

Strangely dad doesn't come on board. The detective waves goodbye to him as he and Matey amble away along the towpath.

Stepping down on to the stern deck, 'Can I have a word please, Mrs Mallory.'

The mist from the canal is enveloping the boat. 'Come inside.' I close the door behind us and open my hand and we sit opposite to each other on the chairs.

While he isn't welcome, as his presence will wind me up, he is only doing his job. 'It has been brought to our attention that you received a death threat yesterday.'

'Did dad tell you?'

He nods. 'I have read the police report of the incident which is brief. Could you fill in a few more details for me? Why would you receive a death threat?'

'I am a journalist and work for a broadsheet newspaper. While I do many articles I am best known as an investigative reporter. My current task is a miscarriage of justice for a case about two years ago.'

'Ah, now I understand. The picture comes together for me. I will escalate the threat to be thoroughly investigated.'

I am mystified by this conversation. Why is he concerned about the threat hanging over me if he is investigating Jasmine's case?

'Have you made any progress on the cause of Jasmine's death?'

'Not that I know. It is still labelled as a suspicious fatality.'

He stands. 'I will keep you updated with any information about both cases. He peers down the passageway to the front of the boat. 'I'm guessing as I cannot hear movement that your husband is not currently at home.'

'He is not, but why do you ask?'

'Purely precautionary. Whenever there is a possibility of a serious crime, we advise everyone involved to be wary of their personal security. I advise you to stay with friends if he is not expected to return.'

Why the sudden concern about my safety? He never offered cautionary advice at this morning's meeting. 'Thanks. But I shall be perfectly safe. Rufus. Here boy.'

The claws on the wooden floor sound as he moves from his sleep in the front salon. He comes at a brisk walk but slows as he notices the visitor. Coming to me he sits next to my legs but watches the detective.

'Take one step towards me before you go.' He only completes a small shuffle forward when the terrifying low menacing growl echoes through the boat.

To be fair to him, he is not concerned by Rufus's aggressive reaction and laughs. 'You have made your point that you have personal protection.'

He turns to go. My mind races and in a moment of inspiration it's obvious that I need to explain the thoughts that have twirled through my mind. 'Don't go, I've joined the pieces together. Please sit.'

He tilts his head to one side but sits down again.

Rufus growls. I stroke the top of his head, 'Lay.' He follows my instruction, but his eyes remain firmly on the police officer.

My stomach turns somersaults. The palms of my hands are sweaty with fear, and I guess I have paled.

'Are you okay, Mrs Mallory?'

I gulp. 'People in the past have confused Jasmine and me. We are similar height and build. We have blonde hair and last night we were both wearing similar outfits that were blue.'

'Please stay calm, Mrs Mallory.'

'Dad, worked it out didn't he, which is why he came to find you.'

'Yes, his old skills from when he was a Chief Inspector have not deserted him. It is most likely a coincidence, but we will err on the side of caution. To be honest, Mrs Mallory while it is described as a suspicious death, by tomorrow the pathologist will have made his judgement. The view of the experienced officers on the case is that Jasmine's death will be accidental.'

16

Abigail has texted to say she will arrive later with Ryan but is unsure of the exact time as they might pop into a pub on the way. With them on board my tension will drain away. Ryan is enough to terrify anyone attempting to creep onto the boat. He's so scary. With Rufus next to me, or more precisely laying on my feet, I have managed to complete some of my journalistic work. I cannot face working on the miscarriage of justice report, so I am preparing a column for a fellow journalist who is on holiday. It surprises me that despite all that has occurred I manage to concentrate. Completing the work, I close the file and intend to watch television until Abigail arrives.

The stomping down the steps from the towpath surprises me. Rufus raises his head but recognising the arrival chooses to return to his doze.

'Jason. I thought you were staying at your mother's tonight.'

'Well, she suggests you should not be left alone.'

'Jason, that is damned well ridiculous, and you know it. Not only am I content on my own but also Rufus is here. Anyone coming on board will get short shrift from him.'

He and Rufus stare at each other. 'I don't think he has ever liked me.'

His words do not come as a surprise, although I have never considered this scenario before. 'You fetched him from the dog sanctuary when we first moved here, as you wanted to feel secure on the boat. Well, it works perfectly. I am secure with him next to me. If you cannot think of a better reason for returning to your home than your mother sent you, grow up and piss off to the pub to watch the football as I've my work to complete as it has been a disrupted day.'

'I'm surprised you can concentrate after what's happened.'

I try to sneer but am not sure what expression I achieve, although it will have no effect on Jason. 'Jasmine's death is tragic and it impacted on me this morning as I knew her well and liked her. But apart from answering questions from the police about mundane matters, I need to move on with my life.'

I am in no mood to deal with Jason's ramblings although the lack of memory about last night's party from overindulgence in alcohol, has hit home. It must have done, as while working in the evening, I always have a bottle of wine open. Not tonight, although I broke my new non-alcohol rule with Benjamin, but I consider that was exceptional under the circumstances.

Jason will be of no help. We will only argue if he stays. I'm anxious to chat to Abbigail as I want to be assured that Jasmine's death has not affected her.

Jason stands with his hands on his hips, and an unreadable expression on his face as he decides what to do. Whether he expected a welcome I cannot be sure. But if he wants to stay, I can hardly kick him out. It emphasises the point for me that within the next few days we need a serious talk. I wonder what his mother said to him. Her arrival at the boat was unprecedented. For the first time in my life, I experienced a camaraderie with Linda.

Darkness has been quickened by the mist that has descended on the canal, as the warm autumn day turns chilly which is a contrast to the previous evening. I am struggling with the last twenty-four hours since the party, when so much has happened.

The rear spotlights on the boat trigger as someone steps down from the towpath. I glance but close my eyes at the sight which appears. The detective has returned. My heart sinks. I don't want to answer any more questions today. I push my uncharitable thoughts aside, as last time he came at dad's bequest. I must give him the benefit of the doubt. Studying me, he grins in a friendly manner.

I don't react. Rufus's rumbling growl fills the air.

Constable Smith has more steel about his body posture and his eyes focus on Rufus. 'Be quiet and sit down as we have met before.' He raises his hand in a flattening motion, 'Sit.' Rufus obeys. I am transfixed by his actions. Dealing with a large dog is not easy as they are protective of their owners and dislike strangers.

Why has he come back? He told me nothing else would happen until tomorrow at the earliest.

Averting his eyes from me, he ignores Rufus who sits watching him. Stepping towards Jason, he flashes his warrant card, 'I am Detective Constable Martin Smith. Are you Mr Jason Mallory?'

'Yes.' Jason pales.

'You do not have to say anything. But it may harm your defence if you do not mention when questioned something which you later rely on in court. Anything you do say may be given in evidence.'

My eyes open wide as I gape at my husband's panic-stricken face. 'Jason?'

But he does not reply nor look at me, but stares straight at the Constable.

'I am arresting you in connection with the suspicious death of Jasmine.'

From nowhere the Constable produces handcuffs. Jason backs away. 'There are two huge coppers on the tow path who will put them on whether you like it or not.'

Jason's mouth moves continually but no words emerge, although he offers his wrists. The Constable duly clips on the handcuffs.

Jason groans.

There are no words to express the shock of my husband, of twenty years, being arrested over the suspicious death of a female neighbour. I slump back onto my seat as the Constable leads him away.

Day Three

17

Giving up on sleep at six o'clock after a torrid night, I crawl from bed. Jason's arrest is unbelievable. Why had they come for him, when by the Constable's admission, they have not received the pathologist's report?

Before retiring for the night, I had phoned Linda. It was important for her to know what was happening to her son. It was a lengthy chat as she was understandably upset by Jason's arrest. In the end I managed to convince her it would be a simple misunderstanding.

Yawning, I stretch and rub a hand across my tired eyes attempting to clear the heaviness from them. It doesn't work. My head aches, my mind is fuzzy and I am listless. It is difficult to summon up any enthusiasm for the day ahead. As usual Rufus is keen for a walk but thankfully only sniffs at his tennis ball in the corner. At least he doesn't want to play in the park as he did yesterday morning. Although it is hard to believe that it was when we returned from our walk the previous morning that Rufus found Jasmine. So much happened yesterday. While today might be less traumatic, I fear it will not be plain sailing. What will it throw up at me?

'Come on, fella. Let's go.' The sunny morning is clearing the last of the mist from the surface of the canal. It promises to be a warm day, so I only need a light jacket. Passing under the cool shade of the trees, I put Rufus on his lead as we are going to walk along the Finchley Road to reach dad's house at Belsize Park. The fresh morning clears my mind and the nightmares disappear into the ether. No amount of thinking can deduce why they have arrested Jason.

As I walk towards dad's house, the worry about him returns. The cardigan yesterday. Although I told him, he still left it misbuttoned. The little hair that he has left was a mess as it hadn't been trimmed or even combed.

His house comes into view. Why does he keep a three-storey house when there is only him? While mum was alive, he always told me that she would never move. But I suspect he won't either. The house is worth a fortune and he could buy something to meet his needs in his old age.

Letting Rufus off the lead he bounds up the steps to the front door. I stand at the gate in astonishment. About a fortnight ago the house had peeling white painted walls, now it is cream and immaculate. What a transformation. I shudder to imagine how much it cost.

Letting myself in with a key, 'Dad, are you there?' I often must shout several times because of the size of the house.

He leans over the banister, 'Up here darling. Come and view the new development.'

I grimace in wry acknowledgement. If he is on the first floor, he is playing with his train set again. A glance towards the kitchen reveals it needs tidying and the hall is desperate for a hoover. I must keep a closer eye on him. One of the reasons for choosing to live on the Regent's Canal is that it is only a short walk to dad's house. I resolve to visit him on a more regular basis. When it is convenient, I shall chat with him about organising more help. A cleaning lady who would come on a regular basis would be a start. Then perhaps I could arrange for meals to be delivered. There are many reputable firms who deliver excellent quality food. These thoughts cheer me up. I want my dad to be cared for and happy.

The large room where he keeps his trainset is the biggest room in the house. It is really a bedroom but he uses it for his time-consuming hobby. Since his retirement he has constructed a complicated model railway complete with sidings, stations and appropriate scenery. While it is detailed and fascinating as the trains whizz around, he appears to be dedicating all his waking time to it.

Climbing the stairs, he waits for me on the landing. His face lights up, 'Hello, darling. I presume you have come because you are worried about the case.'

As he has always been able to deduce what I have been

thinking, this guess is as accurate as usual. But he will never rush and prefers to approach any topic with careful consideration. On hearing voices, Matey appears and the dogs bound backwards and forwards along the landing. They career in an out of the rooms. Dad takes no notice.

With a big cheery grin. 'We will chat in a minute. Why don't you make us a coffee and feed the dogs. I will finish a bit on the new part of the railway.

As dad hasn't reappeared, I carry the coffees upstairs and enter the room where he keeps the model railway. I stop in amazement. He stands beside me and gives a rumbling laugh. 'I thought you would be surprised. It was getting a bit cramped in this room, so I had the builders in to knock a hole into the next room and I'm extending in there. I shake my head in disbelief as he intends to make the layout forty feet long.

'Come through to my study and we will have a chat.'

As usual the room is a mess. Not hoovered or dusted.

He throws the piles of papers from each of the leather wing-backed chairs on to the floor and settles himself. To my relief he has discarded the messy cardigan and is wearing a jumper. No buttons to get confused with today. I glance at his shabby slippers. They are threadbare and the heels are squashed flat. I must insist on a shopping trip soon. Like all men he will grumble but he needs new clothes. A trip to the barbers will also be necessary. These thoughts whirl through my mind as we make ourselves comfortable.

'I'm listening, tell me your concern.'

Tears fill my eyes and run down my cheeks. 'Last night the police officer returned to the boat and arrested Jason.' He rubs the stubble on his chin and his eyes are thoughtful. 'What's happening, dad. I don't understand as the officer told me they will not receive the pathologist's report until today.'

'That will only be the preliminary from the post mortem but it is likely to indicate the tentative cause of death. The police will then know whether there is a criminal case to which they must uncover a solution.

'But Jason's arrest!'

'Patience, darling, I'm coming to that. The police were around all day yesterday, weren't they?

'Yes.'

'They will record statements, such as yours for discovering the body. In addition, they will ask people when they last saw Jasmine. Constable Smith who came with me to the boat was tasked with checking the statements to corroborate them. If he found something which indicated the person was not telling the truth or had left out crucial facts, they would re-interview them under caution.'

'Yes, that's clear dad. The Constable cautioned Jason before they took him away.'

He is thoughtful as he sips his coffee. 'There is another possible reason.'

The first one appears perfectly reasonable. With Jason sporting such a vague mood and often drunk in recent weeks, he has forgotten something crucial and become awkward.

'A standard process is to have a cursory examination of the victim's possessions. That can sometimes reveal a mystery that needs to be solved. For example, had the victim arranged a meeting by text. Unlikely as it was a party, but you understand the idea. If they found a question that needed answering, then they might do it under caution.'

Dad's words are reassuring and make sense. 'What will happen next?'

'They will probably release him after the interview. Depending on what they uncover he might be released unconditionally or put on police bail and have his movements restricted.'

'It will be good news if they release him.'

He finishes his coffee. 'Is everything okay with you and Jason? From the outside the relationship does not appear as good as it used to be. Tell me to keep my nose out of your affairs by all means.' An embarrassed chuckle fills the air.

I manage a nervous grin, but it is forced. 'We've hit a bad

patch, but I am happy to stick with him, but we need some time and space.' He nods but does not appear convinced.

18

Although dad does not accept my explanation about the relationship with Jason, he is confident he will be released. Will that be the time to speak with him? It could help and might put us on a better footing to deal with the turmoil and disruption caused by Jasmine's drowning.

It is mid-morning after visiting dad before I turn onto the towpath in Regent's Park and head towards the canal. I let Rufus off his lead. A van is wedged on to the towpath and is parked where the barbecue had been during the party. Glancing at the logo on the side, Regent's Cleaning Services. Benjamin had indicated that he would engage a company to clean and tidy the boat. A man and woman in a green uniform which matches the colour of the van, carry cleaning implements onto the boat.

Another van, white with no logo, squeezes in behind the cleaning vehicle and Benjamin climbs out. He waves and strides across to meet me as I arrive. Smiling he hugs me, which is unusual as he normally pats me on the shoulder in a friendly fashion. His strange approach unnerves me. Why is he treating me differently today? To my surprise he makes a fuss of Rufus who he usually ignores. Rufus has encountered him many times and is not concerned about his presence and accepts the tickle on the top of his head.

Standing with his hands on his hips, he surveys me, 'I'm much later than planned as the police wanted to question me at length this morning, so I have just picked up the hire van to move my belongings to the new flat.' He appears relaxed and more friendly than customary which is strange as yesterday must have been traumatic for him. He does not show any concern after his interviews with the police which must have been harrowing.

Opening his wallet, he hands me a business card. 'I can't stop now as I only have the hire van for one day, but why not come around for a drink one evening. Despite the circumstances I enjoyed the time we spent together yesterday. Why not come tomorrow evening, as I will be settled in by then and you can update me on the latest scandal?'

'Jason can update you on the local gossip when you meet him.'

'No chance. He won't be invited to the flat. Must go.' He gives me another hug and a kiss on the cheek.

I stand for a moment bemused at his newfound friendliness as he disappears into *Carpe Diem*. Then another question surfaces. Why isn't Jason going to be invited to his new flat? Strange. They have always got on well together. Clutching the mooring rope to steady myself I step down on to *Serendipity* as my mind races. Why the complete change of attitude towards me? While he has not been dismissive in the past, neutral is the best word I can think of to describe his former approach.

Today for the first time he has engaged. Is he thinking that a casual drink at his flat will lead to anything else? His invitation was ambiguous. I resolve to be wary of Benjamin until his purpose in inviting me becomes explicit.

19

Rufus is tired from our walk to dad's house and after a lap of water wanders towards the bow to flop out in the sunshine. Although he will appear to sleep through every eventuality for the next few hours, his sensitive hearing will pick up any sound he does not like. It is a comfort to have such a perfect watchdog.

With him dozing in his favourite spot, I mull over Benjamin's invitation to visit his flat. It is too difficult to fathom out his motive, so I dismiss it from my mind. I stand in the galley staring around in uncertainty. What shall I do to occupy myself until Jason returns or contacts me? More journalistic work is out of the question as concentration with the developments today will be too difficult. Yesterday's turmoil produced results in domesticity, but I do not have the heart to do it again. My stomach twists because under these circumstances I would have popped to the next boat to have a coffee with Jasmine. My stomach lurches.

I must focus on something. Despite leaving a message on Jason's phone he has not replied. Rufus will get grumpy if I insist on another walk. It's time for some serious thinking. Journalism has taught me to start with a small idea and check if it develops and, if not, move on to another small idea. A perfect solution, but how should I begin?

The first one, is tricky. How to coerce Jason into a chat about our relationship. With a coffee that I am not sure I want; I settle at the dining table next to the galley. Should I appeal to his ego and ask for his opinions? Nope, it isn't my style.

The best approach will be to insist he sits down and listens to me. But then what do I say? Should I start with gentle hints as a fore runner to the real issue? I chuckle, despite the overall tension of the situation. Such an approach will not work as he will disappear to the pub before we can reach a conclusion. Why should it be so difficult to talk to my husband of twenty years? I have no idea. Glancing at the clock that hangs at the side of the dining area it is only midday. Time drags when you are in a state of anxiety.

Would a gin help my thoughts to flow? No. I must not weaken. I have given up drinking. It is terrifying that I cannot remember my actions at the party in the latter part of the evening. The beefburger and tomato sauce splattered on my top tells the tale.

Jason appears on the tow path and steps down on to the boat. The tired bland expression on his face reveals nothing of his thoughts. As I am seated, he normally comes towards me, kisses me on the top of the head and moves through the boat to hang up his jacket. His instinct turns his first small steps towards me, but he pauses and shakes his head.

My deliberation before his arrival produced no obvious result.

Without removing his jacket, he slides into the bench seat opposite to me at the dining table with no alteration of expression and no greeting. The change from his normal routine puzzles me. I stare in bemused silence and wait expectantly for him to speak. After a long silence, during which I am almost holding my breath, he lifts his head and scowls, 'We need to talk.'

To me it is such an obvious statement, but I also clamour for an explanation about his arrest by the police. Dad maintained they would have picked up on something contradictory in his statement or new evidence has emerged. The constant stress of not knowing what is happening raises my stress levels and I do not need my morose husband, sitting opposite to me, grunting and frowning.

Taken aback by his words, I want to talk as well. Our relationship can't continue in this hostile and awkward manner. I haven't changed my mind. So, I will tackle him. It's the right opportunity. Steeling myself for the confrontation I draw in a deep breath, 'Over the last few months…'

To my surprise he doesn't allow me to continue but raises the flat of his hand. This is not a good start. 'Shut up, for once in your life and bloody listen.' I wince with uneasiness at the aggression in his voice. Banging his fist down on the table his expression darkens and he glowers. 'I do not need one of your sermons on the mount, exposing my inadequacies again.'

Stunned. I tremble. He never speaks with such aggression even when he is drunk.

Words fail me.

'In your nosey inquisitive manner into my life, you will want chapter and verse about everything that happens when I am not in your sight.'

He can't be drunk as he has only recently been released from police custody where he had been kept overnight. The change of attitude terrifies me. His wide eyes, instead of the usual half sleepy appearance are set against a snarling jaw.

He leans forward, but I move my body away forcing it back into the seat. 'The police picked me up, because they examined the details of the phone messages and texts that Jasmine had sent and received.'

My breathing is shallow and my mind struggles to grasp his new approach. 'What did it say?' I blurt out the words and then realise it is the worst possible question.

'As usual you are bloody incompetent. How does your newspaper employ you to research historical cases, when you cannot perceive what is under your nose? This attribute has always been a mystery to me.'

The penny drops about his behaviour over the past few months. It is blindingly obvious. Disbelief surges through me and it is hard to breathe. Finally, I manage to force the words out, 'You have been having an affair with Jasmine.'

'Yeah, you have finally got there. But I am not going to apologise as she was a wonderful woman and if I find out who killed her, they will be in the canal to join my darling.'

He leaps from the bench seat.

Without waiting, as his aggression and duplicity distorts my ability to think clearly, I leap from my seat and face him. 'You did not want to talk to me, you only wanted to reveal what a two-timing bastard you are.'

Control has deserted me. Rage grips me. I desire vengeance. I smack my hand against his face.

His lip bleeds.

Focusing, he sneers at me with icy contempt, raises his hand and crashes it into my face.

The force knocks me sideways and my head whirls making me dizzy. I land on Rufus. He breaks my fall as he races past to attack Jason, growling menacingly and with his teeth bared.

Bewildered and bleeding from the face wound I lie on the floor. My mind whirls. Jason has hit me. Even under severe provocation, I never expected that. He runs through the stern of the boat to the towpath. Rufus escorts him growling and snapping.

He remains on the stern deck barking. 'Rufus, here boy.'

He comes immediately and lies down beside me. Sitting up. The dining space wobbles as I move my head, but gradually the furniture stops waving around. Blood drips down the side of my face. Grabbing my bag which had been on the seat next to me, I extract my compact and flick the mirror open. The cut on my eyebrow is barely noticeable. My shoulders relax. Head wounds bleed a lot. Pressing a tissue on to my eyebrow, I climb up on to the seat.

Realisation hits me. My marriage is over. I put my head in my hands and weep.

20

An hour later I slump on to the bench seat in the sunshine. The cut is no longer bleeding. After showering I inspected my wounds and applied some make up which covers the minimal damage. What will life without Jason be like? Nothing will persuade me to even contemplate meeting him, although he has been my husband for twenty years. That is a long time. Tears trickle down my cheeks, but I am now calmer and will wait to contemplate what the future might bring. One thing is certain. I no longer want Jason to be a part of my life.

Since finding Jasmine in the water, I have searched for activities to occupy my mind. That must continue as I might easily fall into self-pity as I have been taken for a sucker, by Jason and Jasmine. Benjamin asked me to update the other two boats in our little group about his sudden decision to leave, but I will delay that until this evening after he has gone and the *Carpe Diem* has been locked up.

Thinking about Benjamin, it is now clear why he no longer wants to associate with Jason. He knew of the affair. Is that why he has a different attitude towards me? I push thoughts of Benjamin to the back of my mind. I do not want to dwell on his motives as too many other concerns have invaded my life.

Can I pluck up courage to return to my investigative article about the miscarriage of justice. I have downloaded many aspects of the case from the web but have not read them. Perhaps to read and bring my reasoning up to date might smooth the way back into work and stop thoughts of Jason invading my mind.

The death threat and possible mistaken identity still hang over me. No, I cannot return to the case. It sends a shiver through me just thinking about it.

Glancing up to the towpath, I groan as Constable Smith strides towards the boat. Rufus barks, but I send him away to the bow. I sit on the stern deck in the sunshine and open my hand for him to sit. I will try to act normally.

He doesn't sit and there is no welcoming smile. Why is everyone so solemn and grumpy today? 'We need you to come to the police station.'

These are not the words I want to hear. I roll my shoulders and groan, 'Why? You asked questions yesterday in the caravan.'

Giving a dismissive flick of his hand, 'That has been moved and relocated for a different investigation.'

'Why can't you ask them here?'

'Please don't be awkward, Mrs Mallory. We have difficult topics to deal with. At some point in the interview, which I need to record, I anticipate you will require legal advice.'

A shiver runs through my body which is already weak from the episode with Jason. I have to try several times to catch my breath. Finally, I succeed and after several deep gasps I am ready to speak. 'Can I refuse?'

He grimaces in angry impatience and his eyes narrow. 'You can, but it will put both of us in difficult positions. So please come to the police station and answer my questions.

I'm not just going to accept his request. I need more information before I agree. 'What difficult positions?'

'I must ask you some questions. If you refuse to come with me, I must decide whether to arrest you. If I do, then it will involve a large number of formalities and I anticipate you would be kept in custody overnight.'

'What! You stupid man.' My temper rises, and I wave my arms in frustration, 'I haven't done anything wrong.'

'We must ask you questions. It's your choice. Make up your mind as I've not the time to debate the pros and cons with you. I am giving you the option to voluntarily attend the police station. Now what is your answer?'

My God, I need to calm down so I can think matters through. He is thinking of arresting me. I need help. What questions? What is he going to arrest me for? In custody overnight? That is a horrendous thought.

'I'll come as you are trying to intimidate me and I've no witnesses.' Jumping up from my seat, my head spins and my knees wobble but I will not show him my weaknesses. 'I want a witness in case you try to bully me again.' I give him my best scowl, but his face shows no reaction.

'I will ring ahead for the duty solicitor. She was in the station when I left.'

Locking the boat, I pass by without glancing at him and clamber up to the towpath. 'Come on, let's get this done as I've better things to do than answer your daft questions.'

A person enters the bland room where I have been taken. She is too young to be a solicitor. More like a schoolgirl. 'Hello, Mrs Mallory, I'm Inula Pettigrew, the duty solicitor for this police station. With beaded hair and wearing a flamboyant multi-coloured dress she appears ready for a party. She is supposed to offer me legal advice, but at least she will be a witness if the Constable tries any of his threats or tricks.

Her round black face has a friendly expression, 'You have not been arrested and are here voluntarily. You may choose to end the interview at any time but be aware that the Constable has the right to arrest you. If he does, the interview will stop and you will be formally processed before continuing. Do you know why he is threatening to arrest you?'

'No, I am the person who found the woman from the next houseboat dead in the water.'

The door opens and Constable Smith enters. 'Are we ready to answer questions?'

He does not glance towards me. Inula nods.

He sits at the other side of the table. 'I wish to ask you questions about the afternoon and evening of the party.'

I resolve to keep a dead pan expression on my face and will not respond to any provocation. His statement does not warrant a response, so I stay silent.

'Please consider the timescale between three pm in the afternoon and the end of the party. Did you speak with Jasmine during those times? Can you elucidate about each occasion as it is important for our investigations?

My brain fogs. I can't think clearly. I stare at him in confusion.

'How many times did you chat with her?' The question is barked at me. His voice is sharp.

'Once as far as I can remember when I arrived at the party.'

'Were you on friendly terms?'

'Yes.'

He focuses intently on me. 'I do not believe you are telling me the truth.'

'I bloody well am, you stupid man. Are you trying to trick me? You are trying to stitch me up.' My voice has risen and the realisation hits me that I am shouting at him.

'Calm down, please. Mrs Mallory.' Inula's hand grasps mine. 'Have a sip of water and answer the Constable's questions. I would advise you not to make accusations or to shout at a police officer as it is an offence for which he could arrest you. Take another sip of water.'

The Constable sits back in his chair with an expressionless face.

Inula turns her attention to the officer as I sip. 'Constable, you accused Mrs Mallory of not telling the truth. Could you be more precise in your statement so that she has a more defined context on which to base her replies.'

After several sips, I am calmer and regret my outburst. Although she is like a schoolgirl going to a party, I admire the way she deals with the situation.

The Constable is not pleased. 'Yes, Mrs Pettigrew, I will be more precise. Before the party, I believe you met with Jasmine on the towpath.'

'Thank you, Constable.' A beaming smile transforms Inula's face. I am not impressed with such friendliness towards the opposition as she is supposed to be on my side.

Ensuring my voice stays flat and quiet. 'I forgot about that meeting with Jasmine.' Neither he nor Inula show any reaction.

'What was the meeting about?'

I sigh. 'The positioning of the barbecue.'

'Did you disagree with Jasmine?'

'Yes, we argued, but she would not move it. Benjamin moved it later.'

He glances at Inula. 'The other context is near the end of the party, on the towpath.'

'I do not remember meeting her then. The barbecue incident I forgot, but not that one.'

Inula purses her lips. 'May I ask on behalf of my client how you know about the alleged meeting?'

'We have two signed statements from witnesses saying that Amanda and Jasmine were standing a little distance away from the rest on the towpath and that it did not appear to be a friendly chat.'

'Thank you, Constable.'

She touches my hand, 'Does the Constable's explanation prompt your memory?'

Tears roll down my cheeks. 'No, it does not. On the night of the party, I drank a large amount of gin and can remember little about the party after the middle of the evening.'

Inula's eyes travel back to the Constable. 'Do you have more questions for Mrs Mallory as she is upset.'

'Yes, but I can delay the interview to allow Mrs Mallory to re-compose herself.'

'No please go on. I'm okay,' My voice is croaky, but it's the best I can manage as my throat is tight and dry. I'm not okay, as I am shaking like a leaf and my stomach churns as though I've consumed a bottle of gin.

'Did you arrive at the party with your husband?'

'No, he went on ahead.'

'Did you spend time with him during the evening.'

'No, he was with Benjamin on the stern deck and I was in the galley.'

'Witnesses have stated that the two men had a disagreement near the beginning of the party and were not noticed talking to each other for the rest of the evening and did not remain on the stern deck.'

I put my head in my hands and will my brain to remember the events of the party, but the gin infused fog will not clear. The room is silent. They wait for me to drop my hands.

'Mrs Mallory, when did you discover that your husband was having an affair with Jasmine?'

My eyes open wide. The affair is common knowledge with the police. 'This morning. After you released Jason, he came back to the boat and told me.'

'Did you know of the affair on the day of the party?'

'No, I did not.'

'The behaviour of the four involved, Benjamin, Jasmine, Jason and you requires further investigation as normally, according to witnesses, you are a foursome, who are happy with each other's company. But on the night of the party there was little or no interaction between you.'

Inula touches my hand again, 'The constable has explained a conjecture. I would recommend you do not respond.'

She squeezes my hand and hands me a tissue.

'Thank you.' My mind buzzes. This interview is worrying. What are they implying?

Inula's voice dominates, 'Constable, may I have your assistance?'

'You may if it will help us proceed with the investigation.'

'As I have only joined this case this morning and have no background knowledge. May I assume the questions are leading towards an arrest? And what is the alleged crime.'

'You are correct Mrs Pettigrew we are questioning before, hopefully, coming to an arrest and prosecution. Jasmine was discovered by Mrs Mallory dead in the canal water. The post-mortem has revealed injuries before she entered the water so the charge will be murder.'

'Ahh. You think I murdered her.' The room spins and I hit my head as I fall from my seat.

21

Recovering from my faint, I sit alone in the medical room at the police station. I still quiver that the police consider I am a principal suspect for Jasmine's murder. That is such a shock. I assumed she had fallen and the death would be described as a terrible accident. Through my haziness after fainting, I cannot remember whether they came to any conclusion. In the next few minutes, I will find out although I cannot fault them on the way I was cared for. They had called an ambulance, but I declined to go to hospital.

The door opens and the Constable leads the way followed by Inula and my mother-in-law.

'Linda, what are you doing here?' My spirits lift as it is wonderful to see a familiar face although it is a surprise. Why has she come?

Without hesitation she settles herself next to me and pats me on the arm in a reassuring manner. 'Jason came to visit me after he left you on the boat. He told me he had hit you. I threw him out of my flat and went to the boat. Neighbours told me the police had come for you. So, I came here.'

The Constable and Inula open their eyes wide at the information that Linda has imparted.

'Let me check the two cuts.'

I give a false laugh. 'One on each eyebrow. A matching pair.'

Linda peers closely. 'I used to be a nurse. Yes, they are okay, the paramedics did a good job. Your eyes are fine and your pulse and breathing are okay.' Linda's ability to make such a quick assessment astounds me.

'Mrs Mallory.' The Constable's voice is serious. 'Would you like us to investigate the assault on you by your husband.'

'No.'

'Thank you, Amanda. My son doesn't deserve your support.'

Inula moves closer and squeezes my arm, 'You are in a difficulty with the police here. I can understand why you might not want your husband interviewed but they are not obliged to accept your word. Assault is a criminal offence and the victim does not have a say in the arrest and prosecution.'

'Thank you, Inula, you have been truly wonderful in helping me.'

The deep voice of Constable Smith dominates. 'Mrs Mallory, I have informed the Custody Sergeant that I will not arrest you, but as you, and Mrs Pettigrew understand, you are a key person involved in the circumstances surrounding the death of Jasmine.'

I nod. There is not much else I can do as the situation described by the police appears irrefutable, but I don't want to be arrested.

22

I step down into the boat with a helping hand from Linda. I have a sense of relief that after the interview with Constable Smith I was released. All the evidence led to the conclusion that I had murdered Jasmine because she had stolen my husband. A tremor runs through me. It is and open and shut case to them but I did not murder Jasmine. I will have to prove my innocence.

Rufus bounds out to meet us. I never have to worry about him as dad will come past several times a day and if the boat is locked, he will take him for a walk with Matey and feed him, if necessary.

Trying to rally myself and assume some sort of control. 'Coffee, Linda?'

'After such a traumatic day, I suggest a gin and tonic so we can discuss the way forward.'

The idea appeals to me, but I will only have a small one as I do not need a gin befuddled brain. With shaking hands, I pour far more into her glass than mine and we settle ourselves in the rear salon. Linda's support has been invaluable. It was a revelation to learn that she had thrown Jason out because of his conduct. I never thought that she would take my side against her son.

'I'm hungry.'

It was a surprising admission from Linda.

'I can cook a quick meal.'

'No, what's in the fridge.'

'Tapas style snacks in the freezer such as samosas. I can warm them in the microwave.'

'Perfect.'

Fussing around in the galley allows me to focus on simple daily tasks rather than thoughts of Jason and murder. Another harrowing day, but Inula and Linda have been magnificent. Linda? A mystery. She has always been the distant mother-in-law. Or that is how I perceived her but today under pressure she has come up trumps.

Presenting a wide serving plate full of tapas, as I am sceptical about what she will eat. I slump into my seat. I cannot prevent a sigh. 'You will want to talk about Jason.'

'No. Any mother will support her son, but he has stretched my cooperation to the limit by hitting you.'

'Linda, be realistic. I hit him first.' While I appreciate her support, I must be open and honest.

She tucks into the tapas. 'After I questioned him, he revealed that. He has been unfaithful. You slapped him. He hit you. There is a remarkable difference in my mind. He is twice the size of you. A slap he would hardly notice. The fact that he hit you, is a different matter. Did he knock you off your feet?'

'Yes.' But for some reason I try to hide my reply.

But Linda is ever watchful, her eyes miss nothing. 'To answer your question, do I want to talk about Jason. No, I do not. When he reappears, he will gain no sympathy from me. What you do about him is your choice, but I would kick him out if I were you.'

'That's what I want to do.'

'Then do it. He is not the topic of conversation as far as I am concerned.'

Food and drink must have gone to my head as I have lost the emphasis of the conversation. 'What is?'

'Inula explained the evidence against you. I am not sure what the word is in police circles, but I believe it to be circumstantial. You would never kill anyone. I have watched many times over the years as you have helped a fly out of the window or have ushered a toad off the footpath. Murder Jasmine. No way.'

'Thank you, Linda.' Her faith in me is such a comfort. It's good to have someone on my side.

She fetches the bottle and tops up the gins. 'Constable Smith is a lovely lad but would struggle to battle his way out of a paper bag.' I chuckle at the ridiculous image which forms in my mind. 'Also, the seniors in the police force are not much better if they give him the responsibility. In my day you had to guide and nurture junior nurses otherwise a catastrophe could occur.'

She grins reassuringly. 'You are an investigative journalist.' I nod. 'Imagine being released after umpteen years in prison and running a story about your own miscarriage of justice.'

I shudder, but Linda has hit the nail on the head. I did not murder Jasmine. Someone else did. 'Your support is wonderful.'

She waves a dismissive hand as she selects another samosa from the tapas plate. 'If the police will not come to the right conclusion, we need to organise a team to solve the issue, but trusted people only.

'No, you have lost me, Linda.'

'You, me and your dad, Abigail and her new boyfriend. Perfect team.'

It is too mind-boggling to contemplate. 'Have you met Abigail's latest?'

'She always brings a new boyfriend to meet me. It's hard to keep up but her latest is Dracula, isn't it?' I laugh, which after the trauma of the past day feels good. 'I had an interesting chat with him. Clearly an intellectual, which is what we need on a team. Now we need a plan.'

As I top up the gins, I cannot believe the transformation in the woman that I have known for over twenty years. How did I miss such a resourceful and caring woman? It's terrible to realise that I dismissed her as Jason's mother and made no attempt to form any friendship with her. What an idiot I've been.

23

The first part of the plan agreed with Linda is to talk to those on the nearby boats who attended the party. It is a pleasant evening and I need to walk Rufus. Linda joins us as we stroll along the canal to Regent's Park. Montgomery from the *Green World* boat approaches in the opposite direction, presumably returning from his job in the city.

'Hi, Montgomery. I'm glad we have bumped into you. I wonder if you can help me, as I am in trouble with the police.'

He smirks with self-assurance, 'Of course, I will if I can.'

Linda takes Rufus to play ball but remains within earshot.

'Have the police questioned you about the party?'

'We made statements on the morning after the discovery of Jasmine.' He puts his arm around my shoulder and squeezes. 'Poor you, finding her in the water must have been a terrible shock.'

'Yes, and the horror has not totally passed as the police keep interviewing me.'

'What about?'

'The first was about the discussion I had with Jasmine on the towpath just before the party. The police maintain it was a furious argument, but I remember it as a minor disagreement about the location of the barbecue. I don't know whether you recall the incident as you were around at the time as I waved to you.'

'Yes, I do. I was about twenty yards away and I saw you talking and pointing but there were no raised voices.'

'Would you be prepared to tell the police?'

'Yes, of course.'

'Later at the party do you remember me chatting to Jasmine near your boat.'

'No, can't help there.'

'Did you see much of Jasmine at the party?'

'No. Only in the distance. But I always tried to avoid her as I did not like her.'

'By the way, Benjamin asked me to tell everyone he has moved out and will sell his boat.'

'That's a bit sudden after Jasmine's death, isn't it?'

Shaking my head, 'He stated it was already planned and the party was a farewell do.'

'Sounds fishy to me. I spoke with him at the party and he didn't mention a word about leaving.'

He shuffles from foot to foot making it obvious that he is keen to get home. He waves his hand in farewell, 'I will tell the police about the barbecue if they question me again.'

As Montgomery strides away, Linda re-joins me. 'What do you think of his response.'

'He was lying, but why? I do not know about later in the evening, but early evening I witnessed him having two focused conversations with Jasmine. Did he lie to the police about chatting to her?'

Linda shook her head, 'The police soon detect omissions or lies when they compare people's statements, but as the police have not revisited him, he gave them a different story to what he told you. That's confusing.'

Rufus decides it's time to go home and turns along the path to lead us back to the boat.

My first encounter to elicit the truth about what happened at the party has been an abject failure, but I will not give up because unless the police get the right version, I might finish up being charged with a murder that I did not commit.

Linda touches my arm as we arrive back at the boat, 'We didn't make any progress on the first one, so who is next?' I pop Rufus onto the boat.

'Let's try the quietest couple. Letitia and Russell. They reside on *Kingfisher*. The smartest boat around here.'

Linda shakes her head, 'I don't think that I have met them before.'

'Letitia is an artist and according to Jasmine makes a lot of money from her paintings. Russell is away on business so is rarely here, and I have not chatted to him before. According to the gossip he is the worst type of man. A complete lecher.'

Linda laughs at my description. 'Let's check how they react when we turn up together.'

As we approach the boat, Russell wearing shorts and a vivid green polo top, waves from the deck. 'Have you and Letitia a little time to help us with a difficulty?'

'How could I refuse to help two gorgeous ladies.' The dead pan expression on Linda's face shows her opinion of such comments. With a grin of dazzling proportions, he offers his hand to steady her as she climbs down onto the deck. Then he gives her a welcoming hug which she does not return.

Releasing Linda, he turns to assist me down the steep steps. I am also enveloped in a hug as I reach the deck and he holds on to my hand far longer than necessary. I shudder. Still smiling he ushers us into the rear salon of the boat.

I have never been on their boat before. We rarely meet and when we do it is usually on the towpath.

Wow. What an interior. I pause and allow my eyes to wander over the smart décor which is in sharp contrast to the mismatched furnishings on the *Serendipity*. The rich red leather seats are set in rosewood frames. The subtle mustard yellow inserts are followed through in the curtains and ornaments. Wherever space allows, paintings are displayed.

Russell calls out, 'Letitia, we have visitors, the delightful Amanda and Linda.'

She comes to meet us with a friendly expression. 'Hello, welcome aboard. I left some brushes carefully balanced so I must sort them. But I will not be long.'

Linda is sizing up the room and the two people who she hasn't met before. Linda flashes a charming smile, 'Russell, please explain to me about the wonderful furniture in this room.'

I acknowledge the hint that Linda thinks it's better to separate them. 'Shall I give you a hand, Letitia.'

'Yes, that would be helpful as I wanted to have a private word with you.'

Letitia doesn't notice me raise my eyebrows as I follow her to the front salon. She snatches at brushes that are balanced on the edge of a small trolley filled with her painting gear. Having dealt with that task she turns to face me. 'It must have been traumatic for you to have found Jasmine.'

'Yes, I still have the flash backs, but they will gradually disappear.'

'I shouldn't speak ill of the dead, but I found Jasmine a detestable woman. Even the first time I met her she tried to seduce Russell.' It was a revelation that had come out of the blue. I am only a passing acquaintance so why be so explicit? The depth of our previous conversations have never gone beyond the weather.'

'If you didn't like Jasmine, why did you go to her party?'

She laughs in a false and controlled manner. 'Although she made a fuss about the party with those ridiculous invites, I went because Benjamin invited me. I like him and often talk to him about creativity. It is such a pity he is leaving this little enclave, although we also intend to relocate soon.'

'That is a disappointment as I thought you enjoyed painting the local area.'

'We've been planning it for about three months, ever since several of my paintings were stolen.'

'I didn't realise, that's terrible.'

'That was the second time it has happened, and we are giving up and going for somewhere more secure. Shall we rejoin the others?'

Without waiting for a reply, she leads the way through the boat to where Linda is edging towards the exit.

'Many thanks for your time and the tour around the boat.'

Linda grins at Russell. Unusual, after her reaction when she first met him. 'Russell didn't observe the incident with the barbecue or you chatting with Jasmine later in the party.'

Russell comes to help us from the boat, but Letitia remains inside.

Linda goes first and while she slowly climbs the steps that are more complicated than our boat, Russell catches my hand and leans close. 'Now that you are on your own, as Jason has left, would you like a discreet drink at a local pub.'

Bad news travels fast. How did he know Jason had left me? Not wanting to alienate him in case we need more information I do not verbalise my concerns. Instead, I eye him with a friendly expression, 'If I do, I will let you know.' Catching my hand to steady me up the first two steps, his other hand squeezes my bum.

We return to the boat and step inside before we both burst out laughing. 'What did you think of that, Linda?'

'Unbelievable. Within ten seconds of you going to the front of the boat with Letitia he made a pass at me.'

'Did it upset you?'

'No, not at all. But he was less enthusiastic after I told him that I would do him a mischief which would stop his Casanova activities for several months. He didn't touch me after that.'

I laugh. 'Are we making progress?'

'None. What do you think?'

'I agree.'

'Hi, anyone there?'

The soft lilting voice is distinctive. 'Come in, Samantha.'

'Hi, girls. Montgomery mentioned that you are anxious for information concerning the party. Can I help?'

While she has come to offer assistance, I am apprehensive as I have never enjoyed her company, although we have not spoken a great deal. Her manner is often confrontational, and she tends to be outspoken. In my view she is rather overconfident.

We settle on the seats near the dinette. Linda smiles towards our visitor, 'Poor Amanda has been having a terrible time with the police especially over the relationship between her and Jasmine.'

'That bitch.'

The venom in her words surprises me.

Linda chuckles. 'I gather from your comment that you didn't like her.'

Samantha's face tightens and her nostrils flare. 'It wasn't

long after we moved in about a year ago that I came home from work early as I was feeling weak with an onset of a cold. Montgomery had taken a few days holiday to redecorate the boat. For once, I was wearing soft soled shoes. When I reached the lounge. Jasmine, naked above the waist, was in Montgomery's arms and had her hand inside his trousers.

My eyes open wide, as I did not expect Samantha to be that explicit.

The intensity in Samantha's face is obvious and she grins with a flash of arrogance. 'One fault I have and it is the only one I will admit to, is my temper.'

'What happened?' I blurt out the words as intense curiosity sweeps through me.

'Like any normal person discovering your lover in the arms of another woman I took the appropriate action.'

Linda stares intently at her, 'You stormed out.'

Samantha laughs and pats the back of Linda's hand. 'Dear, sweet lady, that would be the best action, but not for me. I attacked them, but I couldn't decide who I wanted to hurt the most, so I hurt them both. Both would have struggled to have sex for about a month.' She throws back her head and laughs. 'In the end they crawled off the boat but not before I had thrown Jasmine's bra and jumper into the canal.'

'But you are still with Montgomery. Did you finally forgive him?'

She gives a dismissive flick of her hand. 'We have not slept together for a year. The boat is sponsored by our company and we have a generous entertainment budget for purveying green ideals which is compatible with the increasing range of herbal teas we sell. Customers come to examine our business to discover how we include green practices into our lives. It would cost a fortune to buy our current lifestyle, so we shelved our problem and agreed to continue to live rent free. She stops and peers around. 'Amanda, where's Jason?'

I shrug and raise my eyebrows, 'Hasn't the news reached you?'

She laughs again which is not a characteristic she displays often. 'No, but the way you are glancing at each other means it is serious.'

'My son has left Amanda after having an affair with Jasmine.'

'Bloody hell. That has put the cat amongst the pigeons.'

Day Four

24

Rufus's acute sense of smell must have sniffed gin in the air yesterday evening when I chatted with Linda. So, he decides I must require fresh air at six thirty in the morning. Dog logic continues to confuse me. The non-drinking regime I had promised myself has not happened, but I have been successful in resisting the urge to drink too much. So far, I have not reached the personal debacle of the party.

I have no fear of going anywhere with Rufus. He has demonstrated over the dramatic days since Jasmine's death that he will be next to me. Although waking me at an unearthly hour, he ignores his ball on the stern deck, for which I am grateful, and leaps up to the tow path. For some reason he remains by my side this morning and does not bound ahead in his usual manner.

Plodding along the towpath, I try to shake the sleep from my head. The amount of gin, while it is not beneficial, should not have an impact on my day, although a six thirty start wasn't on my agenda.

Generally, he likes usual routes when he is left to choose. To my surprise he turns towards Little Venice. It is rare to go in this direction, but I have no reason to complain and dutifully follow his preference. I wave to Montgomery on *Green World* as he opens the doors. Rufus growls. I tap him on the head as he walks along side of me. No doubt about him growling when anyone steps onto the boat but he rarely does it when out for a walk, especially as no one has come near me.

The gin infused discussion with Linda was good, but we have made no progress on proving my innocence. We decided that even if we could identify the killer what could we do about it. If the murderer guessed we had found him or her, then what would they do? Two more bodies in the canal? Although dad wasn't there yesterday evening, he would have urged us to leave it to the police. We concluded it would be a wise move.

We reach Little Venice, which is not far, but after a few sniffs, Rufus turns around and heads for home. He's in a strange mood today. The first sunshine of the day peaks through. The previous few days were traumatic, so I hope this one is calm. Why we have turned around after a short walk I do not know. I sigh. Why am I trying to work out dog logic when I cannot get a firm handle on my own logic.

As we approach *Serendipity*, I plan a day to make progress on the death in the cemetery as the assignment deadline is drawing ever closer. Shall I continue with the desk-based investigation? Possibly, but the descriptions in the court proceeding of two years ago were explicit on the location of the murdered man and the killer. Apparently, it is an unusual cemetery, so the relative positions are important. I want to visit to consider my own view. But will that happen in time for me to write my article for Toby? I don't know as the shocks of the last few days have overwhelmed me.

The sight of Constable Smith striding down the footpath, causes my stomach to twist with apprehension, a sensation I do not enjoy. Judging by the pace we will meet on the towpath near to the boat. Drawing a deep breath, I nod a good morning, it's all I can manage as the sight of the man affects my ability to speak.

'Good morning, Mrs Mallory.' At least his tone is relaxed. 'I want to update you. The circumstances of Jasmine's death are being revised. The initial conclusion was murder but subsequently the full report stated that the death required further investigation, so the police have downgraded the enquiry.'

It is good news, but it does not mean that I am no longer a suspect, and that supposition will continue hanging over me like a dark cloud. 'Will you explain further why the police and medical support have changed their views?'

'No, that is confidential information.'

I scowl in disapproval.

He raises his eyebrows in amusement, 'Talk to your father, he will explain without knowing the details.'

That is not the answer I want. Dad can only guess, which will be a valuable insight, but Constable Smith has the details. He is an infuriating man. I step towards the boat, and he acknowledges the hint and returns along the footpath.

Planning my day ahead I will not attempt to replicate the police investigation but will continue to meet people with a view to gaining more information about Jasmine. She was only a loosely tied partner to Benjamin, had an affair with Montgomery and broke her relationship by embarking on an affair with Jason. How she related to Russell is a mystery but viewing Jasmine's generosity with sex, and Russell's proclivity to chat up any woman, a liaison between them would not be a surprise. Was any man safe in her company? She obviously like to spread her favours around.

Intrigued by the change in the police approach I intend to meet with dad later but will start with Benjamin as he is the one closest to Jasmine and the police might have given him more information. Rufus is happy to be left on the boat and heads towards his favourite position on the front deck.

My mind drifts as I walk the mile or so to Benjamin's new flat. It is early, but he has often been up on the boat long before a normal breakfast time and he probably won't change his pattern because of the move to a new flat.

Pressing the buzzer on the outside of the plush new three storey block of flats, I receive a signal as the main door opens.

Taking the stairs rather than the lift I tap on the door of Flat Eleven. Benjamin opens the door and his handsome face has a friendly expression. 'Great to see you, Amanda, come in. Coffee is on.' The hug which follows the kiss on the cheek carries on for much longer than I expect. When on the boats he was never a tactile person. Why the change? He hasn't mentioned Jason's affair in any of our meetings since Jasmine's death. Is the alteration in his behaviour towards me because he knows I am now unattached. This thought depresses me and I push it away.

His breath smells of alcohol. While he might be suffering from a hangover as he is a heavy drinker, for the smell to be detectable in the morning is unusual.

He leads me through to the kitchen and indicates a stool at the breakfast bar. The flat is bright with magnolia paint throughout. The kitchen and furniture exude quality pine and the worktop of black granite glistens under the down lighting.

'Have you received any updates from the police?'

He places a mug of coffee in front of me and gives a false laugh. 'Update is perhaps the wrong word. A police officer visited last night and told me the suspicious death will take longer than normal to investigate but he refused to give me further details.'

'Much the same as I received from the police this morning. Later today I intend to speak to my dad who will understand the possible reasons for the delay. Shall I pop back if he tells me anything of interest?'

Shaking his head, he averts his eyes and stares down at his mug of coffee, 'No. Nothing is going to bring her back, so I want little information about the police actions as it just prolongs the issues.' He licks his lips several times as he continues to stare at his coffee.

'Are you okay, Benjamin?'

He lifts his head and forces a smile. 'I coped with her death while on the boat but since I have moved here, I have found it more difficult.'

'Is there anything that I can do to help?'

He inhales deeply. 'Yes, please, Amanda. It's a task I have found too difficult.'

He wrings his hands together and then gulps down some coffee. 'When I moved from the boat, I dumped Jasmine's clothes and belongings in black plastic bags expecting to sort them out later.' He gulps and his hand trembles as he picks up the mug of coffee. 'But I've not plucked up the courage to go through them.'

'If you want me to take them and do it for you, I am most willing.'

'Thanks, Amanda. I appreciate your help.'

He comes around the bar and kisses me on the cheek. Again, I can smell the alcohol on his breath. The increased tactile approach gives me a cause for concern. The invitation to visit him at his flat had been ambiguous.

'What shall I do with her clothes and belongings after I have sorted them out?'

'Give them away to charity or bin them, it is up to you. I do not think there will be anything of value in her belongings.'

'Okay. I will check whatever is there and make a judgement. I will return any items of value to you.'

'Thanks that will be perfect.'

'As returning to the boat might be too traumatic for you, do you want me to check that the cleaners have left everything in order.'

'Yes please. He crosses the room to a drawer and passes me the key to the boat. He sways as he moves, indicating that the alcohol must have been consumed this morning. It's still early. Has he been up all night? How does he manage to write so well? He is often drunk and incapable in the evening along with Jason. It does not make sense.

As he is leering at me it is time to leave. 'Give me the bags and I'll leave you in peace.'

He leads me to a bedroom that is unused. Three large bin bags lay on the bed. 'Can you manage?'

'Yes, no problem. I'll pick up a taxi.'

25

Dumping the three black bags under the stairs on the entrance to my boat, I resolve to sort through them in the evening when I will have time, as I do not expect visitors. My mind buzzes with the change of approach from Benjamin. The death of Jasmine has affected him.

On the afternoon following Jasmine's death, he talked freely about her without becoming upset, whereas this morning he was struggling to control his shock and despair. When we had sat on his boat, he had emphasised the relationship had been one of convenience, but today's reaction was the opposite. He missed her. Their decision to split was not indifference on his side but due to Jason's affair.

The nagging thought keeps returning. When does he write? Reflecting about his previous habits, he was often moving around the boat in the mornings or out on the towpath chatting. In the evening, he was often drunk. The afternoon for writing? How long does it take to write a book? Working only in the afternoon will not produce one quickly. Setting up my laptop, I search for him and his books.

A quick flick through the info provided by the publishers, a major company with a good track record does not produce any useful clues.

In an inspired moment, I ring for an immediate appointment, have a quick change of clothes, and catch a taxi to Bloomsbury.

Stepping from the taxi, I enter a white painted Georgian terraced house with the publishers' brass plaque indicating it was Braithwaite and Jenkins Publishing Company. The traditionally furnished entrance with embossed cream wallpaper and a thick cream carpet leads me to reception.

A young lady in a smart white blouse sits behind an ornate oak desk.

'Good morning. My name is Amanda Mallory. I have an appointment with Mr Braithwaite.'

'Yes, I will show you in.'

She stands, opens the door behind her and after announcing my name ushers me inside.

The overweight, short man with grey hair and a blue suit, shakes hands. 'How can I help you?'

'I am a journalist and Toby, my editor, is considering a series about authors.'

'I know Toby and would welcome an article about many of our authors, did you have one in mind.'

'Yes, I do. We live next to each other on canal boats along the Regent's Canal.'

'Benjamin Foster.'

'I haven't mentioned it to him yet, as we are in the preliminary stages, but wanted to delve into his background to check out whether there is interest for our readers.'

'I'm not sure about scandal.'

'No, that is not the angle I want to pursue. It is about writing and what inspires him.'

He grinned, 'I can definitely point you in the right direction with his inspiration.'

'You can. Excellent.' My spirits rise and I fix my face into a friendly expression.

'Benjamin went through a bad patch with his writing style deteriorating and the number of books he produced was falling behind deadlines. We were becoming reluctant to offer him further contracts.'

'Did that change?'

'The inspiration resurfaced when he moved to the canal boat. He had once told me that he had planned out several books so knew where the series was going. Suddenly the change happened. He produced books at a much faster rate, and they required far less editing. Quite a transformation. And the only change in his life had been where he had chosen to live.'

It was not the only change in his life at the time, not that I would reveal the other one to Mr Braithwaite. What influence did Jasmine have on him?

26

My life stands a chance of returning to normal, although I will be on my own, as I will not have Jason back in my life. My visit to Benjamin's Publishers did not directly reveal Jasmine's involvement in his writing, but it remains a possibility. No amount of thinking can confirm what happened to Jasmine and why? I will suspend further consideration of that until I sort through her clothes, although I cannot imagine that it will help me or the police to discover her killer.

The disruption of the past few days has not helped me write the account of the miscarriage of justice. Although it is an impossible task in such a short time scale, I will attempt to pursue the first stage of my investigation. I have printed out the location of the church, cemetery and where the body was found but want to visit the site to gain my own impression. Toby will expect a suitable description of the graveyard to introduce the article. I can complete that today while I research into the court case.

'Hi. Are you there, Amanda?'

Recognising the deep well enunciated voice, I climb up to the stern deck. 'Hi, Montgomery.'

He steps forward, embraces me and kisses me on both cheeks. Dressed in his usual style of long grey shorts, matched with a strange fluorescent tee shirt with eco symbols. His outfit is completed by flashy orange and green trainers which exhibit a well-known logo.

What is happening to the men around here? Benjamin and Montgomery have suddenly become more tactile. Does he behave differently if Samantha is not nearby or perhaps he fancies his chances now that Jason has abandoned me. Stupid man. He is not my type. All that enthusiasm for green issues puts me right off. Plus, I do not find him attractive. His eyes are an insipid shade of blue, his blonde hair is rather floppy and his face is only weakly handsome.

Breaking away from him, I drop onto the seat, 'What can I do for you, Montgomery?'

The voices wake Rufus and he climbs the steps to the deck and keeping a careful eye on Montgomery, he flops onto my feet.

'You are much brighter today, Amanda, but it must be hard for you coping with the multiple traumas and changes in circumstances that you face? Samantha and I are finding the stress of the enquiry going on for days is affecting our sleeping and we want nothing more to do with it. I have been interviewed by the police again, but I told them no more questions or assistance in the future. The police want to bring up background information which is best forgotten. You asked me previously if I would help. I did for a short time, but I want the matter to drop and recommend you do the same.' He shuffles in his seat and avoids eye contact by studying the towpath, which is empty. Rufus's eyes remain fixed on him.

Why the sudden change of approach? Has he something in his background that he does not want brought out into the open? Is he hiding information from the police? He's scanning me and his eyes are now focused on my breasts. Before long he will make a pass at me. No chance. But he doesn't know that yet. I have no intention of telling him the different stance that is being adopted by the police.

'I have noticed you visiting the other boats, it strikes me you are keen to keep the stress going.'

Shaking my head, 'You are wrong, Montgomery. I've a pressing deadline for my work. Did you read the introduction a few days ago?'

'Yes, you will investigate a miscarriage of justice.'

'Yes, it is a murder in a cemetery that will be my focus for today. I shall visit the site and make some notes.'

He is worried and is keen to warn me off. Intriguing.

Shivering, I force myself to observe my surroundings and scribble notes. Although the sun is out the cemetery is still and sinister. In my mind I expected a row of gravestones, some neatly tended, and others overgrown separated by grassy paths. But the reality of this cemetery is different. Two huge grey mausoleums block the view. Muddy paths between the monuments, many of which are taller than me produce hidden niches which fill me with apprehension. Rusty metal railings around several graves impart a claustrophobic sense of entrapment. According to the reports the victim often slept on a bench at the back of the church. I locate it at the end of the path near the entrance to the catacombs which are found under the church. Nothing would induce me to contemplate sleeping in this area, but it was the setting for the murder.

I wander around the area to avail myself of the situation, I can write a scintillating piece about the graveyard which will rival a description of Highgate. Why would a young woman of eighteen volunteer to tidy the surrounds of the church in such an environment? Arranging the flowers in the church is okay but outside is a different matter. The crime was committed in December so the low light would have created a more haunting atmosphere in the churchyard with a multitude of shadows.

Wandering through the area, I glimpse a flash of brightness. As far as I am aware there is no one else in the graveyard. The eerie enclosed landscape holds enough terrors. The flash of brightness hits me again. Green, fluorescent. I saw it earlier this morning. Montgomery. Has he followed me? I'm sure I am not imagining it. My logic kicks in for a change and I assess the relative height of the person sneaking next to the monument. I have no doubt whatsoever. It is Montgomery.

I decide to ignore his presence and enter the church, where I will make a quick assessment for my story. The flowers shine out in the cold, austere, stone environment. Is the flower display the continuation of the norm after the murder? Does someone else now come to this gloomy spot to refresh the flowers. I shiver. It's not a task I would be prepared to undertake. The haunting environment is too much for me. My nerves escalate and I make a hurried exit from the church and almost run to the entrance of the churchyard. Panting, I scamper down the road. I will get a taxi home.

It is strange to enter the boat knowing no other person is there. Rufus in his usual style comes to meet me. A small tail wag, while he stands waiting for the tickle on the top of his head. Judging by the bowl on the floor, dad has popped in and fed Rufus. He's so thoughtful.

Grabbing a quick bite to eat from the fridge, I am anxious to write up my notes on the visit. Tomorrow I will receive a progress call from Toby, and he will insist on an update. While a good guy he does not accept deadlines being missed. If he commits the newspaper to a story he expects a result, otherwise my job might be on the line. He has a ruthless reputation for sacking journalists that do not deliver.

It's already late afternoon so I will write the atmospherics for the article this evening. The luminous green tee-shirt at the cemetery persistently returns to my mind. Did Montgomery follow me? What did he hope to achieve? Why did he try to warn me off pursuing any further information about the party? I shake my head at all the problems which rattle through my mind. Too many questions but no answers.

Although tucked away out of sight, the black bags of Jasmine's possessions intrigue me. But I must make progress on my journalistic article as the timescales are becoming ever shorter. An idea flashes into my mind as this in-depth investigation involves too much time which I don't have. I have never involved my dad in cases before, but he might provide a crucial interpretation. I will send him the press cuttings and many details of the case that I have found, with a quick note. *I am under pressure on this one can you help.* How will he react? Grimacing as I press the send button I fear a reprimand, which I will accept.

What should I do first?

The answer appears loud and clear as Rufus brings me his ball.

'Come on boy, let's go. Lead the way.'

He bounces from the boat with enthusiasm and we head along the towpath towards Regent's Park. As it is afternoon other people might have occupied his preferred space but as we arrived the area is reasonably free, so I throw the ball.

Montgomery's appearance at the cemetery has unnerved me as I cannot come up with a logical explanation for him to follow me. My mind continues to search through the possibilities between the endless throwing of the ball. Montgomery is trying to distance himself from the murder investigation. Why? Did he kill Jasmine? Discretion was not one of her attributes. For an affair they needed to be away from the boats, but the description by Samantha of the encounter resurfaces in my mind. He was fully dressed when she burst in on them. She was top half naked with her hand in his trousers. It suggests that she instigated the encounter. Her motives are difficult to judge with any accuracy. Montgomery was at the party. Did he seize the opportunity and deal with Jasmine? I shall be wary of him, but as dad would say I am creating a story with no evidence apart from hearsay. It is a valid point.

Rufus returns with the ball and lays down. It's his usual sign that he is ready to go home. Patting him on the head, we turn towards the canal. As we amble along the track, he enjoys exploring the long grass and vegetation which borders the path. Although he is often out of sight, I do not worry as he will follow in his own good time. Devising his own route, he usually times it to arrive at the boat at the same time as me. Uncanny. But I am used to his ways.

I stand to one side as a group of boys on bikes come racing along the tow path riding fast but also pushing each other and shrieking with laughter. Amusement flickers through me. Oh, the joys of youth. Facing each day in a carefree manner.

As I meander, I ponder Jason's affair with Jasmine. If she had lived, would it have been renewed? Who knows? I push the thought aside as useless and unprofitable speculation. It doesn't matter. My mind drifts back to the latest meeting with Montgomery and his requests for me to cease my local enquiries and stop hassling everyone. I still can't understand what he hoped to achieve by following me. I cross the bridge to join the towpath and pass through the heavily wooded section where the mist often lingers. Today is bright, and there is no mist but with the trees in full leaf it is gloomy under the overhanging canopy. All is quiet. There is no one around. Pausing I turn to locate Rufus.

The sudden heavy impact on my back knocks the wind from me. Struggling, I am unable to keep my balance.

The canal water is icy cold. Gasping. I sink and gulp in mouthfuls of water making me cough and splutter. Air. I need air. My brain screams at me to push myself to the surface, but my clothes are weighing me down. Gasping. The water covers me again. My arms thrash. Survival. But which way? My sense of direction has deserted me. Darkness is all around me as I sink down once again. The water becomes turbulent. A solid object is nearby. I grasp it. Air. The single word repeats itself over and over again. I need air. I am now on the surface of the water. I splutter and fill my lungs with fresh air. I will make it. Rufus is next to me. I am clutching on to him as he swims towards the side of the canal. People are on the bank. Through my bleary eyes I glimpse Montgomery nearby. 'Help me.' I splutter as I cough and spit out the foul-tasting water. Rufus knows I am safe as Russell and passers-by grab my clothes to stop me sliding back into the water.

People on the tow path drag me from the canal and place their jackets over me while Russell rushes off to *Kingfisher* and returns with several towels. I sit on the ground for several minutes feeling disorientated and shaken. With unsteady legs I finally stand and thank everyone for their kindness. Tears fill my eyes as Russell helps me back to *Serendipity*.

Rufus is next to me. The dog has the uncanny notion that people like Russell are helping but he watches every movement. Russell smiles, 'Shower and change while I make you a cup of coffee and pour a brandy for you which will warm you and calm your nerves.'

The shower helps and the warm dry clothes make a difference. I am no longer shaking but I still suffer from shock at the terrible encounter. As I walk unsteadily into the galley,

Russell gently catches onto my arm and helps me through to the seat in the bow. The sun is shining through the windows. The salon is hot which is perfect to quell the occasional shiver. The coffee and brandy warm me. Russell does not make himself either a coffee or pour a brandy for himself but instead sits and watches me with a concerned expression.

'Thank you, Russell. You are kind to help me. Did you observe what happened?'

'No, I was tidying the stern deck on my boat and heard a scream then saw you in the water. Did you slip?'

'No, someone pushed me hard in the back. Although I was not near the edge, I could not regain my balance and plunged into the water.'

'I raced along the bank not sure of how I would reach you. I cannot swim. But your dog came racing along the path and with a tremendous leap landed close to you. You grabbed him and he brought you back to the side. It might have been those kids on bikes as they have been intimidating everyone this afternoon. I shouted at them, but only received abuse.'

Noises reach me from the stern deck. 'Ah, here is Linda. I shall leave you to her company.'

I lightly grasp his hand as he stands. 'Thank you, Russell.'

A half smile forms on his lips as he waits for Linda to step into the lounge. 'Poor lass we have just fished her out of the canal. She needs someone to sit with her until the shock of the accident recedes.' With a cheery wave of his hand, he disappears.

Linda eyes me with concern. In her usual fashion she peers closely at my face.

'I'm fully recovered apart from the nervousness of the shock.'

'Did you slip?'

'No.' There was no way I could avoid telling her the truth. 'Someone pushed me hard in the back.'

'Have you called the police?'

'No, I didn't see anything, and I am sure there were no

witnesses so what can the police do? Russell was on his boat but saw nothing. My scream attracted his attention. Rufus jumped in and helped me to the shore.'

27

I doze in the sunshine after Linda leaves. When I wake, I lie back on the lounge seat enjoying the warmth of the late sunshine. What a strange but busy day. This morning's visit to Benjamin was different as his behaviour towards me has changed. Then the visit to his publisher which was confusing as he was convinced canal boat living was the key to Benjamin's increased productivity. I remain sceptical. Could Jasmine have been the catalyst? An unanswered question. At least for the moment. Is Benjamin a suspect if her death proves to be murder? Yes. Despite their intended split he cared about her. How much help did she give Benjamin with his novels? Can he manage without her?

Earlier today Montgomery acted strangely when he came to call on me, and then I am sure it was him in the church yard. But why was he following me? Could he have trailed me into the afternoon and waited in the woods knowing I would pass? A fanciful notion. Positioning and hiding would be too difficult. The push held the hall marks of a spontaneous opportunity but by who, Montgomery? But Russell was nearby.

As I lie there in the sunshine. My mind drifts. After my ducking in the canal, Russell behaved like a perfect gentleman. Plenty of opportunity in tucking the towels around me to touch me up. But he didn't. When Linda and I visited his boat, he grasped the opportunity and took a handful of my bum. It's too confusing.

Rousing myself I move to feed Rufus as dad arrives. Has he come about the notes I sent him about the death in the churchyard or is it a normal drop in from walking Matey.

After kissing me on the cheek, he slides into the bench seat of the dining area. 'Linda rang me about the incident when you fell in the canal. I rang Constable Smith but neither of us believe there is anything to pursue.' I can accept their approach.

Placing a cup of tea in front of him, he studies me with a concerned expression, 'Are you okay after your ordeal?'

'Yes, dad. The shock is gradually dissipating, and I feel fine in myself.'

'You sent me the details about the case you are investigating.'

'Yes, I don't normally involve you in my cases, but I am up against a deadline and the distraction of Jasmine's death has preoccupied me. Do you think you might help?'

I expect him to decline, but he chuckles which is a surprise. 'You want me to help you investigate the case? Did you know that an old friend of mine led the investigation?'

'Oh, dad, I didn't realise you knew him as the case wasn't in the area you worked.'

'I remember Jack well as we started as young coppers together.'

'Oh, sorry. I shouldn't have asked. Do you still meet up with him?'

'Sadly not, I attended his funeral last year. If he was still alive, I would have introduced you.'

'That would have been scary as I've never met anyone involved in the previous investigations apart from peripheral witnesses.'

'Jack was an easy going guy and would not have taken offence. I would be surprised that he would have allowed a case to proceed to court and through to sentencing if he suspected something was wrong.'

'Will you answer some of my questions? It might help me realise a way into the story much quicker.'

'I'll have a biscuit before I am grilled.'

'The lass is twenty years old now but was eighteen when convicted. She had a reading age of eight.'

Dad munched on his biscuit, 'Are they the crucial facts for a newspaper to whip their readers up into a frenzy.'

'Yes.'

'In the police we become sceptical about people's ability good or bad. Their outward impression may not reflect their capabilities.'

Dad studies me with a twinkle in his eye. He expects

me to pick up his point and apply it to the case. But I am confused.

I lean back in my seat and eye him with amusement. 'You need to explain as I have lost the thread of your argument.'

'A lass is diligent at school up to the age of sixteen and when she leaves has a reading age of eight. She would have been in special needs classes through the latter part of her education.'

'Is there another interpretation?'

'A lass is a troublemaker from the day she enters school and exhibits severe discipline issues up to about the age of eleven. After that age, she truants and rarely attends school. Both leave with the same reading age and no qualifications. One is naïve and the other worldly wise.'

Taking a deep breath, I try to consider counter arguments. 'But why would the worldly wise one be doing the flowers for the church.'

Dad grins but remains silent.

'Don't do this to me, dad.'

Amusement flickers in his eyes, 'Because her dad was a churchwarden and he paid her. It's in the papers you sent me.'

I hesitate. 'The school records were not in the papers.'

'No, I agree, but the police would have accessed them.'

'But arranging flowers? Worldly wise? They do not fit together even if she was being paid.'

'If she never did exams, there would be no record of whether she was creatively talented. And the victim? Why did he frequently sleep there? He never went into the church. He did not have a record and is that because he did not commit a crime or avoided being caught.'

'Yes, I can understand your line of argument, dad, but it makes my investigation more complicated.'

He grins at me in that endearing way of his, 'All murder cases are complicated and the real reason only emerges from the backgrounds of the people involved and especially the victim.'

28

Alone on the boat I worry about possible intruders, but my protector lies next to me. What would have happened if he hadn't dived into the water? I shudder to imagine. Many dogs enjoy playing in the water, but in all the time I have owned him he has never ventured into the canal. Tickling the top of his head he is such a reassuring presence.

Pulling the blinds and settling as the mist descends, I will try to deal with a number of issues that are outstanding. I must think about my article as dad provided his analysis, which deserves respect but will not stop me writing an article about it, but the stance may be difficult.

Despite gathering all my notes together, I cannot concentrate on the article this evening. Paying bills. After agonising I pour a glass of red wine as I endeavour to sort my finances and complete my work expenses.

Opening my laptop, I log on to the area where I manage bills and money. The amount of available cash in the current account is ridiculously low. I have not overspent during the past few months to warrant such a decline. No holidays. No extravagant spending spree. My mind drifts back to the previous months. The amount in the main account might be wrong, but under pressure from work I just paid the bills with a promise to myself to investigate next month. I've tolerated the situation for quite some time. What is the issue? Has my salary not been paid? There is no alternative, I must investigate although I can summon no enthusiasm for the task. I bring the bottle of wine to the table and douse some of the lighting. Rufus adopts his favourite position of laying on my feet. We are content for the investigation.

The footsteps sounding on the stern deck as dusk settles sends a shiver coursing through me. What is he doing here? Jason's foot thuds are unmistakable. Rufus rouses from a dead sleep at the noise and brushes against my legs as I rise to meet Jason. He still possesses his key so might or might not let himself in. Opening the door removes the decision away from him.

On the steps down into the boat is not a place to start a conversation. With no acknowledgement, I walk to the salon at the bow of the boat as Rufus brushes against my legs. His attendance is reassuring. He will not leave me.

I decide my approach. He sits down in his own home. Fetching a beer from the fridge and a pint glass I place it in front of him. He barely nods but pours the beer. I retrieve my wine from the dining area and return to my seat with what I hope is an expressionless face.

My insides twist and turn at treating my husband of twenty years this way, but I can feel no compassion, only irritation. It should be anger, but the man that I had once loved deserves to be heard which is why I resolve to listen.

He sits silent which is his way. In the past, I would chatter to him but not tonight as I need to find out his reason for coming. I have no doubt that Linda will have made it clear to him, what she thinks of the current situation.

Sipping his beer as though in a thoughtful discussion, he makes different facial gestures that I have observed over the years. What ventures through his brain at such times?

'Why have you come, Jason.'

'To discuss the future.'

'Okay, carry on.'

Following our usual pattern, he would expect me to air my view first, but not tonight.

'Is there any chance that we could reintegrate, meet a few times, before having me back under certain conditions.'

Incredulity washes over me. My eyes widen and I fold my arms across my chest before I utter the single word. 'No.'

'You are harsh to dismiss twenty years of marriage because of a slight dalliance.'

'Crap. Jason and you know it. You wanted another woman and made your choice. There's no returning. You burnt your bridges. Our relationship is over.'

'Mum maintained you would adopt that approach.'

'No Jason, don't try to bring third parties into the conversation this is between you and me.'

'Will you seek a divorce?'

'I might do. But they cost and my bank account is down.'

'But you live here and I do not have anywhere to live.'

'Live with your mother.'

He gulps the rest of his beer. 'We are entitled to split the proceedings of our marriage.'

'Given that I bought the three flats we have lived in since our marriage and this boat I don't understand how you can complain although I concede the courts might decide differently, but I'm in no hurry to go to the money ripping lawyers.'

Standing, his eyes glow with savage fire and he glowers with discontent. Without another word he storms out along the passageway, onto the stern deck and then up to the towpath with Rufus a close attending escort.

I slump into the dining seat after checking he is no longer in the vicinity. Why did I choose that approach? I can give him a substantial sum with a simple solicitor's letter. He will then be out of my life. It was the approach I intended to follow when he appeared. Why do I allow myself to be drawn into a confrontation? An amicable tactic would have been more sensible even though I do not want him back in my life.

I sit in silence with Rufus at my feet. The realisation hits me that I no longer love Jason. When did that happen? I suppose it's been coming on gradually. My marriage is over. I have made my choice and must now face the future alone. It is not a comforting thought. Tears fill my eyes and I bury my face in my hands and sob.

29

Rufus is barking and his pounding paws running the length of the boat wake me. The clock shows it is a little after two o'clock. Why is he barking? I rub my hands across my face as I try to clear the sleep from my head. Something or someone has agitated him. He races again still barking, as I slip on a pair of jeans and sweatshirt. Whatever he has discovered needs my attention and urgently.

Something must have happened on the canal as the boat is rocking far more than normal. Flinging back the curtain, the shadows outside move. I concentrate. The view from the passageway window is different to normal. The realisation hits me. The boat is moving. A sickening wave of terror wells up.

Forcing myself into action I rush to the rear, throw open the door and climb the steps to the stern deck. The sight that greets me fills me with horror. The boat has drifted away from the mooring. The ropes no longer hold it against the bank but trail in the water. The boat rolls forcing me to grab hold of the door to stop myself from falling. With no power *Serendipity* skews slowly towards the far bank.

The night is dark and I need to illuminate the area to start the engine. I locate the torch from the storage area and clamber with increased urgency to the stern deck. I grip the lugs on the hatch but cannot lift it. It is stuck. I swear and kick it in frustration. It's imperative to open it to start the engine. Dropping back to the seating area I crash against the side as the boat lurches, blown by the strong wind that sweeps across the canal.

Grabbing a metal tyre lever, I race back up the steps and try to persuade the hatch to open. The lever slips and I crash my hand against the base of the stern seating. That hurt. The impending danger spurs me on as we are now crabbing down the middle of the canal. The boat is out of control and a strong gust of wind could change its course and we might collide with another residential boat moored at the side of the canal.

Ensuring the lever has a firmer footing I use all my strength to force the hatch open but to no avail. The hatch remains firmly closed. The chugging of a boat engine fills the air. Standing I peer across the dark water and glimpse a boat moving towards *Serendipity*. There are no lights on my boat. I flick on the light nearest but the weak beam will serve little purpose. The advancing boat could hit *Serendipity*.

I must do something. Standing on the stern deck I flash the torch and wave frantically to attract their attention. Then drawing in a deep breath, I shout at the top of my voice. 'No engine. Adrift. No engine.' I repeat the words over and over.

They must have heard me as the engine of the boat slows. A large man waves. 'Do you need help?'

'Yes. No engine. Hatch jammed.'

'Okay, understood. There are two of us on board. We will help.'

A sigh of relief floods through me as their boat slows. A man comes down the side to the bow and waits until the boats nearly touch. 'If I throw you a rope can you secure it?'

'Yes.' I scream back at him with a wild note of hysteria.

The large muscular man throws a rope which cascades onto the stern deck. Grabbing the end, I tie it in with fumbling fingers. 'Secure.'

He shouts, 'We will reverse up, and manoeuvre the two boats so they do not collide with the bank.'

Their engine races and slowly both boats move to the middle of the canal. I grab onto the wooden structure of *Serendipity* to steady myself. It is obvious they intend getting the boats broadside to each other.

It is lucky the pair are experienced with long boats as it could have been a disaster if they were holiday makers with little control over their boat. With the two guys pulling the boats gradually come side to side. They tie the sterns together.

'Coming on board.' The big man waits until the boats rock in unison and steps across and to the side and then on to the stern.

'Hiya, darling. I'm Ricky. When did the engine last run?'

'About six days ago.'

He grabs the lugs on the hatch, but they resolutely refuse to budge. His mate passes over a much longer metal lever than the one I had attempted to use.

With skill Ricky positions it and the hatch opens. 'Looks okay.' He leans into the space and presses the ignition. After a few flutters the engine springs into life.

The sound is music to my ears. What a relief.

'Do you want me to put it back into the berth?

'Yes, please that will be a great help as I do not manoeuvre it often.'

They disconnect the rope. 'The other man shouts across, 'I'll manoeuvre to the canal side past *Kingfisher,* while you position this one back on its mooring.'

Ricky skilfully guides *Serendipity* back to its berth, 'Hey, Dave you need to come and examine this.'

What has he observed?

Dave strides along the bank and grasps the ropes thrown to him by Ricky and secures them into the mooring loops but doesn't use the normal ones. 'They can be retied later.'

Ricky focuses on me, 'Are you on your own on this boat?'

'Yes, only me and a dog. Rufus chooses this moment to appear. His uncanny understanding shows no animosity to the two men although they are strangers.

With the boat secure back on its berth Ricky steps up to the tow path. They both bend over and examine the ropes and have a muttered conversation which I can't hear. Ricky waves a beckoning arm towards me, 'You'd better come and view this, lady.'

I clamber up to the towpath with Rufus next to me, struggling to control my apprehension.

Ricky points, 'The mooring ropes have been cut. The remaining pieces are still tied to the mooring hoops.'

I gulp. Panic surges through me as this is another incident directed against me. Jason was here a few hours ago, but he would not have cut through the ropes. But if he didn't, who did?'

'This is mindless vandalism. If you ring the police, we will stay as witnesses until they arrive.'

'Thanks, guys. I am eternally grateful as your skills averted what could have been a nasty accident.'

Day Five

30

The horror of the incident the previous night when *Serendipity* had been cut loose from her moorings did not invite a restful night's sleep. As usual when I want to laze in bed, Rufus has a game of ball in mind. Tired and sluggish, I stretch and let out a long slow yawn. Although it is not what I want to do, of course I will concede. We plod along the towpath in the grey cloudy morning and he rushes around in his normal excited manner. As we approach the darkened section under the trees where someone pushed me into the water I call him, as I want him as an escort.

Reaching the park without mishap I mindlessly throw the ball until my arm aches. Finally, he sits next to me indicating he is satisfied and is ready to return home. We start on the walk back. A person is standing motionless at the side of the path under the darkest part of the trees. Apprehension grips me. Is someone waiting to push me into the canal again? My muscles stiffen ready to run and I tuck Rufus in close to me. Why is someone loitering there? I expect to view joggers and walkers in the early morning but not someone just standing there.

Hesitating, I want to be certain that I can pass the dark shape. 'Mrs Mallory, it's Constable Smith.'

Inwardly I groan, but at least he poses no danger.

'Good morning, Constable Smith, are you looking for me?'

'Yes, I wanted a word.'

I am dubious that it will be that brief as he will want to talk at length but perhaps he possesses information that will solve the current problems.

He keeps scanning the footpath. 'Is this where someone pushed you into the canal?'

I grimace at the memory and an icy shiver sweeps over

me. 'Just here where I am standing.' At least he appears on my side as he inspects the area nearby although I have no idea what he expects to uncover.

He shrugs, 'Let me check the mooring.'

I lead him back to the boat. The cut pieces are laying on the stern deck. After the police during the night had investigated, they retied my boat to the most suitable loops. He picks up one and examines it. 'A sharp knife, but it is not a quick job as these are thick ropes. Was anyone on board with you last night?'

'My husband visited but didn't stay.'

His brown eyes focus on me, 'Animosity?'

'Some, as we have recently separated.'

'Because you found out about the affair with Jasmine?'

'Yes.' But I don't offer any further information.

'Seems reasonable.' I don't need his endorsements on my action, so I do not comment.

He slumps onto a stern deck seat. I sit opposite. 'Death threat, pushed into the canal and boat set adrift. What do you think, Amanda?'

As it is the first time that he has used my first name I guess he is not intending to arrest me. 'I don't know even if they are connected. The push into the canal could have been an accident from the young lads.'

'No. We received several complaints about the havoc they caused for a few hours. A patrol picked them up, lively lads from good homes. I don't think it is them.'

'Do you think it is related to the death of Jasmine?'

'I've an open mind, the other aspect is the case for your Sunday newspaper. Have you made any progress?'

'None at all, although I've not had much time to pursue it.' I will not mention dad examined it for me.

He gives me a quizzical expression, 'As it was a big announcement, what happens if you get nowhere?'

I laugh and he smiles for the first time. His face is a definite improvement when he is happier. 'The article will be written as a series of questions, accompanied by doubts to highlight whether the answers that were provided at the time, are the correct ones.'

'You create doubt even if you cannot unearth any evidence, but I suppose that's the style newspapers desire.'

'That's a cynical view of journalism.'

He laughs again. But then his face returns to the serious dead pan image that he exhibited during most of our encounters. 'They are a warning to you. I have little doubt. But what about I do not know. I would recommend you do not stay on your own on the boat. The warnings might become increasingly dangerous.'

'Yes. After last night's terrifying ordeal, I will ensure that I am not alone.'

'As your husband is gone, will you go and stay with your father?'

'No. I will persuade my daughter and her boyfriend to stay.'

'Good idea.' He stands to leave. 'Take care of yourself please, Amanda.'

It was said with genuine feeling which surprised me.

31

As Detective Constable Smith departs, I mull over his visit. To be fair to him he links the incidents together but does not have a solution. Neither do I. The death threat. I shudder as I cannot consider it lightly as it is my demise it is talking about. It had been sent to the paper before I found Jasmine floating in the water. The remembered image sends an icy shiver straight through me.

Did the murderer want to distract the attention away from Jasmine's death? No, too complicated. Let me stick with the known. The two issues are separate. One is a nutter. The other the death of Jasmine. I'm assuming it was murder, although the police are not saying. Why implicate me as opposed to the other people who attended the party?

The shock hits me and I sink down with Rufus flopped on my feet. Does the person who killed Jasmine think I saw something that might implicate them?

I groan. Worthless speculation. It will get me nowhere. Be on my guard. Follow sensible precautions. Finish the article about the death in the graveyard which will reveal no development so that threat will disappear, I hope. In the company of others, pass through the weeks until the police reach a conclusion on Jasmine's death.

Life will become normal again, apart from no longer having a husband. A future alone is not an exciting prospect. I push the thought away. The alternative is to allow Jason back into my life. That is not going to happen. No way.

It is imperative to write a decent article for Toby at the paper. I will need to think about it even if I have made no progress as he will be able to spot an article which is lazy waffle. He might go with it to fill the pages, but I will not receive any further commissions and my bank balance is not brilliant so I need to work. The thought comes back to the examination of my bank accounts. I must sort out what I perceive as discrepancies, although the bank might not agree with my findings.

I ponder through the actions that I had agreed. I promised that I would sort Jasmine's clothes and possessions.

The discussion with the publisher comes to mind. Pure speculation on my behalf. After the meeting I clutched on to the idea that Jasmine had ghost written Benjamin's latest novels.

Focus. Sort Jasmine's clothes and then check *Carpe Diem* as I promised I would do for Benjamin. Shifting Rufus from my feet, he will be happy to lay in the morning sun as I visit Benjamin's boat. He is within shouting distance if needed.

Dropping into the rear end seat of the narrowboat, I pull the three black plastic bags from the cupboard under the steps and slit them open.

Clothes fall out. Two piles, one for the charity shops and the other for the bin which would include the underwear. A pile of jeans. Virtually new, the charity shop can mark them up and enjoy a good profit.

I'd better check the pockets. A scrappy piece of paper with Constable123 makes no sense so I throw it in the bin. Another piece of tightly crumpled paper. Spreading it out on the floor I peer at the miniscule writing on the receipt. A Chester art gallery. Four thousand pounds. Why would Jasmine sell her paintings in Chester? Why not choose a closer location? Studying the receipts, it lists in the small print a branch of the business in London. There are also many till receipts from a coffee shop near Paddington station.

Then it strikes me. I have never viewed one of her paintings. Perhaps Benjamin took her stored ones with him, but they were not displayed in his flat. Perhaps it was too difficult as she had died, and he will sell them.

Job done. Clothes separated and bagged for the charity shop. I niggle about the receipts and Benjamin's silence about the paintings. There is nothing in her personal possessions. Where is her phone? Simple answer. Benjamin has dealt with it.

To clear the last of the actions from Benjamin I went via the tow path to *Carpe Diem* to check it through. The company employed had done a thorough job and it is clean and tidy. Checking all the cupboards and cubby holes, I discover nothing. As a last place I check the storage space under the stairs leading to the stern deck. Nothing.

Closing it, I picture the space. Far less compared to *Serendipity* as I managed to store three big black bags. I open the cupboard again and while it is empty it appears much smaller. I ferret around with my hand on the bottom space which was the biggest by far in *Serendipity*. The floor lifts. A laptop and a phone.

Jasmine wasn't a person to be hanging on the end of a phone. Could I remember her using one? No, they are part of modern life and not noticeable, but I also never saw her using a laptop. This could become complicated. Taking the laptop and mobile back to *Serendipity*, I will have a quick check before passing them on to Benjamin.

Rufus is sunning himself as I flick opened the laptop. A piece of paper stuck with Sellotape to the area above the keyboard displays two sets of numbers which I recognise as a sort code and account number. Jasmine's? Probably and careless about leaving the number lying around although the laptop and phone were hidden.

I cannot deal with the investigation now as an appointment at the bank is imminent to sort out the issues with my account.

32

Breathless I arrive outside the bank just before my appointment. Taking a deep breath, I compose myself for what might be a tricky interview. They might doubt my intentions for requesting information, but I will try to be persuasive as I want to avoid them concluding that there is a security issue.

With purpose, and I hope exuding charm, I push open the door and enter the bank. An employee not behind a screen sits at a desk labelled General Enquiries.

'Good morning. I have an appointment to discuss my accounts. I am Amanda Mallory.'

'Come with me please.' He leads the way to a glass walled room and settles himself behind the desk and opens his hand for me to be seated. 'I'm Kevin. How may I help you?'

He does not appear old enough to be employed by a bank, let alone have an advisory role, but I fix my face with a friendly expression. He is a young man and can perhaps be charmed.

'I want to open a new savings account.'

After studying his screen for a few moments, he eyes me with a puzzled countenance. 'But you already have one.'

'Yes, but I wish to divide my savings for two specific purposes.'

'A wise move as it keeps money well organised.' A hint of amusement flutters across my lips and I grin reassuringly. While he is young, he speaks like a bank manager of twenty years ago. 'I will complete the formalities so that you have access to the new account before you leave.'

'Thank you. That is my main purpose for attending the interview, but as I am here could you help me on two other matters.'

'I will if I can.' He appeared hesitant at the beginning but with a simple task to be completed his voice gains confidence.'

So far, so good. He's relaxing.

'I've been checking through my current account and

there is one direct debit I cannot remember.'

'Do you think it is a fraudulent access to your account?'

'No, I am convinced it is not, but I must have set it up a long time ago, as the reference does not give me any clues. If you could prompt me, I would appreciate it.' I pass him the reference.

He flicks at his computer key and glances at me, but I already have the look of encouragement waiting. 'It was set up four years ago. The amounts have increased several times over that period.'

I keep my relaxed and friendly expression in place, 'Can you tell me the name of the recipient as it is not on the direct debit.'

'That is unusual. The amounts are paid to Jason Agnew.'

I give a short laugh which I hope sounds genuine. 'Of course. I forgot about him. A distant relative. I agreed to help him set up his business.'

It is hard not to frown with annoyance, but I force myself to remain outwardly cheerful and hope it comes across as genuine. I never agreed to the direct debit. I guessed the recipient would be my husband. The same first name and he used his mother's maiden name. 'That's cleared that up thank you.'

It was the explanation for the deficiency in my account. With a struggle I maintain a relaxed countenance. I will reflect on his stealing my money and decide my actions later.

'And one final point. I wish to pay for some products I received and have the sort code and account number, but the computer asked me for the name.'

'Do you not know the company you wish to pay? It could be a scam.'

I force a wide smile. He probably thinks I am a grinning idiot, but I don't care if I get the rest of the information I require. 'No, it is not. I know the lady personally and she gave me some items, but I wish to pay her company. If you could tell me the company name, please. My contact is Jasmine.

After several clicks with the mouse, he lifts his head

with a satisfied gleam in his eyes, 'The correct name of the company is Jasmine Enterprises.'

I wait to check whether he will mention about the owner dying. But he makes no comment, so I do not raise the matter.

33

Desperate to make progress on my miscarriage of justice report, I seize the opportunity and arrange to meet with the vicar of the church at the centre of the murder. The newspaper is going through a difficult time and Toby has already made some staff redundant and I do not wish to be in the next bunch. It is important as my marriage has failed and I will need a steady income to pass through this period in my life.

The taxi drops me at the church gate. As I walk slowly through the cemetery, I check behind to ensure that I am not being followed. Montgomery in the bright green top had been amongst the gravestones and monuments on my last visit. Why did he follow me? Another mystery. If he stalked me home on that day, he was a prime candidate for pushing me into the canal.

The vicar asked me to meet him at the church. The fifteenth century limestone edifice must have survived many turbulent times in its history, and I didn't doubt that it would survive the revival of the murder investigation.

Pushing open the door. I enter the chill interior with the sun beams casting a myriad of multi-coloured lights across the nave. A man of about my age, tall and thin with smart grey hair walks down the aisle to greet me. A pleasant smile. 'I am Stephen Phillips, Vicar of this parish.'

'Amanda Mallory.' We shake hands.

Opening his hand, 'Shall we sit in the rear pews. I gather from your request to meet and from the announcements in your newspaper that you wish to produce an article about the murder in this cemetery.'

'Yes, the newspaper believes that there is a genuine reason to reconsider the case.'

He shows no facial expression and sits waiting with his hands in his lap.

'Did you know Tracey well?'

'I have known her all her life. When I came to this parish over twenty years ago as a young vicar, she was one of the first christenings I performed.'

In my hurry I must have missed that piece of information. This article is going to be a disaster, and my job will be on the line. 'How did you get on with her? I believe she did the flowers in the church.'

'A lively girl and then young lady. Helpful in the church and the parishioners liked her.'

I am achieving nothing with bland questions. I must try to be more precise.

'Did she truant from school in her teens?'

'Only a little but I am afraid that the education systems failed her.'

'In what way?'

'I am no expert but she was dyslexic and yet was never classified and given the support she needed. Her reading was slow and poor and her spelling of even simple words inconsistent. But she was outgoing and chatty. She had a good voice and would sing loudly when she had learnt the words.'

Dad was right. It was necessary to dig behind the labels assigned to people.

'Did you know the victim?'

'Yes. He was often in the graveyard but never ventured into the church. Although he was known to sleep rough, I never met him when he was drunk. Why he visited the churchyard I never discovered.'

'Did he hassle any of the female parishioners?'

'Not as far as I know. They all spoke with him not just to bide the time of day, but many would talk with him but elicit very little information.'

'So what did they talk about?'

'The flowers, trees and shrubs of the churchyard.'

I was getting nowhere. A drunk who women avoided was expected.

'I believe you found the body.'

'I did. Have you read the details of my involvement in the court notes?'

'Yes, but a brief description and summary would be helpful.'

For some reason, I didn't expect him to answer my request.

'Intending to go for my lunch, I walked along the path outside to return to the vicarage. As I turned the corner. Michael lay on the floor with a knife in his chest. Tracey sat on the ground next to him with blood on her hands. I dialled 999. Then sat next to Tracey until the police arrived.'

Could it have been someone else that had left, and Tracey found him?

'I can perceive from your face that you think the police might have missed something.'

I frown with a mixture of bewilderment and tension. This interview is not providing any new information.

'Let me add that Tracey was observed by several people to enter the vestry, pick up the knife and walk through the church. I left the church about three or four minutes after her.'

'Thank you for your time, Vicar.'

Leaving the church. It is difficult to understand why the attack took place.

Who in the paper decided that this could be a miscarriage of justice? Someone read the emotive facts and considered them worth further investigating, but they were wrong. Both the victim and murderer are a mystery. Michael by choosing to be in the cemetery and sleeping rough and Tracey by her actions whether planned or spontaneous.

34

Choosing to travel back to the boat by taxi after my chat with the vicar, I flop back into the seat with a loud sigh. This article is raising my stress levels. It's an impossible task. Wallowing in self-pity I stare unseeingly out of the window as we speed through the London streets. My mind buzzes with exasperation as I have nothing to write for the article on Sunday. Normally I would have scribbled into the night based on an idea or interpretation. In my view I have been sold a dummy story by the editorial team. It suggests they are desperate. The reasons for the killing and the mystery of the dead man remain unexplained, but both will have been explored by the police. I must speak with Toby at the paper as even writing a filler is impossible and he will expect a big article.

My phone rings. Should I answer? The number is not in my contact list. No point in avoiding issues. 'Yes.'

'Mrs Mallory?'

'Who wants to know?'

'This is UCH.'

'The hospital?'

'Yes.' A tremor runs through me, I hope it is an insignificant contact.

'Your father was admitted to the hospital this afternoon.'

'My God, what is wrong with him? What's happened? Is he unwell?' The questions pour from my lips as panic engulfs me.

The voice cuts across me, 'Mrs Mallory if you will allow me to explain.'

I sink back on the taxi seat and clutch my phone with trembling fingers as I struggle to control my breathing.

'He has been admitted after an assault.'

I want to jump in but must listen.

'He is comfortable and not badly hurt but will be in discomfort because of the bruises. However, as he was unconscious for an unknown period he will be kept in for observation.'

All rational thought goes out the window and I cannot think. 'Can I visit him?' I blurt out the request although the response is immaterial as no one is going to stop me seeing him.

'Yes, he is still in Accident and Emergency but will be transferred to a ward overnight.'

'I will come immediately.'

'That will be fine and you will receive an update. Good afternoon, Mrs Mallory.'

I spot him at the far end of a room where people on trolleys are awaiting attention. He is sitting up which gives me some relief after the frantic taxi ride where my imagination spiralled out of control. His face is pale but that is reasonable, and he isn't connected to an array of machines which is a relief.

'Dad! Dad!' I wave frantically as I rush towards him. He glances in my direction with a faint smile. 'How are you? What happened?'

'Calm down. I'm okay. I was mugged on Hampstead Heath. Because I fell and banged my head the ambulance brought me here. Since my arrival they have given me several drugs for the pain caused by the fall, but they have made me drowsy.'

My initial agitation subsides but dad in hospital is a big worry and not one that I need. Mugged. I must think as it is essential to support him. After such a traumatic event he will not have considered the implications.

'Can I obtain the details of your credit cards at your house and I will arrange for them to be cancelled. Have the keys been stolen? If so, I will organise to have the locks changed.'

'Just relax, Amanda. My wallet and keys are there in the bedside cabinet. Nothing was stolen.'

He takes a sip of water from the cabinet.

'A mugging?'

'Don't worry about what it is labelled. Unfortunately, I

was in the wrong place at the wrong time. Whoever it was thought I would be easy pickings, but they must have been disturbed.'

He will not make eye contact. There is something in his manner that is elusive. Why won't my brain engage. I am desperate for clear rational thought.

A tea trolley arrives. Dad accepts one and selects a biscuit. He is not badly hurt but disorientated from the drugs. Staring at him my brain finally engages. Right. I have pieced the events together and I now have a better understanding.

He sips his tea and munches his biscuit.

'Dad, the attack on you is related to me, isn't it?'

'Why would you think that?'

'A mugger would steal your wallet and possibly keys. If it is not a robbery, why did it happen?'

He sighs. 'Yes, I cannot disagree with your logic. It's purely precautionary but can you warn Linda.'

I rattle through the connections. If someone attacked dad because of me then the same might happen with Linda.

'I want you all to be safe and would prefer you, Linda and Abigail to stay at my house. The security is good and apart from my office and the trainset room everywhere else including the bedrooms are managed by a service agency. You do not know but many of my friends from the railway enthusiasts club stay regularly.'

It is news to me, but I am concerned about my personal safety and as I wish to ensure Abigail and Linda are also protected it appears a good idea.

'Should I ring Constable Smith and tell him?

His eyes twinkle with amusement. 'He has already been to visit me.'

35

After speaking with Linda and Abigail they both agree to meet up at dad's house this evening and are prepared to stay for a day or two. It might be nothing, but I cannot have any attack on them on my conscience. It is because of me that they require a safe haven.

Should I explain to Linda that her son has been filching from my account for years? No, it is unlikely to help the current situation and might make future meetings between her and Abigail awkward, especially now I have split up from Jason.

In the couple of hours, before we meet at dad's house, I intend to return to the boat to pick up some clothes and examine Jasmine's laptop and phone that were concealed in the cupboard. I'm sure they won't reveal much, but why the secrecy?

While alone on the boat, Rufus will be with me. My first task is to take him for a walk but in my current state of mind I do not enjoy the stroll along the towpath. All the time my brain whirls through the different issues facing me but I cannot reach any conclusion. After feeding Rufus and armed with a cup of coffee I place Jasmine's phone and laptop on the dining table. The information obtained from the bank about the sort code and account number sellotaped to her machine, refers to Jasmine Enterprises. The plot with her thickens.

Unsure I will achieve any progress; I start with the laptop. It has a mains cable with it, so I plug it in and turn it on. Password flashes onto the screen. I thought it would defeat me. The piece of paper in her pocket pops into my mind. Constable123. I try and it is successful.

Scanning the file directory my eyes open wide. The recent titles of Benjamin's book each with varying drafts are neatly listed. She was ghost writing for him.

A subdirectory shows a list of paintings which mean nothing to me, but one title catches my eye, *Seascape in Suffolk*. I love visiting an old aunt in the county who lives by the coast and the seascapes there are stunningly beautiful.

The next directories each refer to the local residents on the boats. I click on mine fearful of what it will reveal, but the subdirectory is empty.

With trepidation I move to the subdirectory labelled Jason Mallory. It contains a series of photographs nothing else. I click on the first one. Jason and Jasmine naked, posing for the camera.

I don't want to view any more. Uncharitable thoughts twirl through my mind about Jason. After viewing those photographs, I want to kill him. But I will not. I just do not want him to be a part of my life anymore. Removing the direct debit that has been a source of money to him will hit him hard. Serves him right. Filching money and pretending to be my husband reveals what a lazy, deceitful, self-centred man he had become. The date of the photo reveals six weeks ago. But to divulge that revelation to anyone else would be a humiliation.

Struggling to concentrate after the explicit revelations about our marriage I want to crawl into a heap feeling sorry for myself. My sense of failure is overwhelming.

Should I disappear for a few months and advise only dad and Abigail about my location. No, I can't. Dad was attacked because of me and Abigail might be targetted. I will stay and uncover the source of the threats as it will not have come from Jasmine as she is dead. There is someone else out there who is targetting me and wants me.... I hesitate before I allow the word to form. Dead?

But now is not the time to think about me. Dad and Abigail and also, Linda must be protected from the danger that is enveloping us.

What else is on this computer? Enough has already been revealed to agitate me. Why would Jasmine have kept files on the residents?'

I will investigate them at a later time but will check anything else of interest before shutting down the computer and moving on to dad's house.

The icon shows a major bank. I press it. The login details have been documented in the file. I log on.

It opens to reveal several accounts but the one that catches my attention has over a quarter of a million pounds in it. Before I have a chance for any further investigation the familiar charming voice of my daughter reaches me.

'Hi, mum. Are you there?'

The arrival of Abigail during this worrying period dominated by turmoil and threats is overwhelming. Gulping, I shut the computer down and stuff it back in the cupboard. I will retrieve it later.

'I'm here.'

Abigail's pale anxious face reveals all, 'What's happening mum, granddad is in hospital and grandma tells me dad has left. I don't understand.'

I envelop her in a tight embrace. 'We need to sort out a few issues.' I did not answer her question about understanding what was happening as I didn't know.

Ryan looms behind her. It will be difficult to have a serious in-depth conversation with Abigail when her boyfriend is here. It cannot be helped as I have no reason to ask them to separate as much as I want to have a one-to-one with my daughter.

'Mrs Mallory, shall I walk Rufus? Come here boy.' Just like the previous time they met he responds to him with a slow lazy wag of his tail. He picks up the lead and Rufus sits. How does he have control over an unfamiliar animal?

'His lead is there, and his ball, treats are in the cupboard.' I breathe a sigh of relief as I want privacy with Abigail.

'Just the lead will do. I shall run with him; he will enjoy it.' How he would run in his long overweight overcoat on a warm evening I won't question as I want him to depart as soon as possible.

The sound of his steps leaving the boat prompt us to wrap our arms around each other. We hold the embrace for a long moment. When we separate, we both have tears in our eyes.

Clutching her hand, I guide her to the seat in the rear salon and slump down next to her. My heart races. I must choose my words with care as the split from Jason is a sensitive topic. Rational thought fails me. No words present themselves and I stare at her lovely face with bewilderment.

'Mum, I met with Dad earlier as he messaged me and asked to speak with me face-to-face.'

The alarm bells ring as I had expected to explain the breakdown of our marriage to Abigail but had Jason got in first. What would he say? I have no idea how he would approach the separation.

Catching her hands, I gaze into her face and while I urgently want to speak, I swallow my words. Her lips tremble and her eyes fill with tears, as she gives my hands an encouraging squeeze.

'I'm sorry mum, I don't believe what a bad daughter I have been.'

I blink several times in confusion. What has prompted her to say such a thing? 'Darling, you are a wonderful daughter, I don't understand. Can you explain?'

Taking a deep breath, she stutters but no words emerge. With wide eyes she continues to clutch my hands as though she is frightened I will escape. It's obvious she wants me to speak. But I can't as if I breach the wrong topic the link might be broken. She fidgets in her seat indicating her unease.

Can I think of any words to explain? No. I can't. All that fills my mind are the usual pacifying words of a parent, which in the circumstances are totally inadequate. Her face is intense but shows no animosity to me.

Drawing in a deep breath she fixes her eyes on me, 'Dad stated that you and him had been experiencing a few problems over the past months. Thinking back, I had noticed some friction, but I dismissed it, as I was more interested in going to Uni and meeting new people. I should have done more to help you both. Afterall, you have been married for twenty years.'

The figures reverberate through me like a shock wave.

Twenty years of my life. What had happened to the man I married?

'My darling, it certainly is not your fault that my relationship with your dad had deteriorated.' This will be a traumatic session but it must be faced. 'Did your dad explain why we have separated.' I realise that I have used the word that she has not referred to, but she shows no alarm.

'Isn't separated rather a strong word, Mum? He hopes that when the issues of money and living difficulties blow over you might try again.'

The despicable toad. He siphoned away my money and embarked on an affair and tries to blame it on a breakdown in the relationship with the hints that there were faults on both sides. Although anger bubbles up I push it away. I shall have a chance in the future to tell Jason some home truths.

'Darling. I must be honest, but as you love both me and your dad it will be difficult for you and a shock you will not like.'

She is wary as she glances down at our interlocked hands.

'Jasmine died after the party.'

She grips and gulps. 'Why do you want to talk about the party?'

'Bear with me darling. I implore you. It's bad news.'

'Okay. The police took a statement from me, but it was trivial as we spent most of the night in the pub. We popped into the party to say hello, as that is what you asked and then went back to the pub who had a late-night licence.'

I have no option; it is essential to reach the crucial point. 'The police asked a lot of questions. I was interviewed several times as I was at the party throughout.'

Abigail does not release her grip on my hands. The tears stop and she puts her head on one side in a quizzical manner.

'Oh mum. It must have been desperate, but why are you telling me this as we are talking about you and dad.'

'After your dad was questioned, he came back here and told me that he had been having an affair with Jasmine.'

Her eyes open wide but show no other reaction which concerns me as she processes the information. I wait. She needs to verbalise her thoughts.

'Will you divorce him?'

I must be honest. It's the best approach. 'I expect so as I will not have him back but will try to let matters settle so that the upheaval does not impact on you.'

Rufus bounds into the boat and sits beside me for his expected tickle. Ryan looms, 'Does he need another walk?'

Subtle and sensitive. I appreciate that. We both shake our heads.

Day Six

36

It is strange waking up in dad's house after all these years, but it is a sensible approach to gather everyone here. The boat is too insecure and with the escalation of attacks it is better to have us all together. I would be devastated if anything happened to Abigail or Linda.

The atmosphere when we settled yesterday evening after a visit to dad in hospital was tense. Linda's face showed the result of the quiet conversation she had with dad, who emphasised she needed to be at his house. While she could accept his concern, the tension showed about a world of violence and threats that she did not understand.

After the news I had imparted to Abigail she was rightly tearful and on edge, but Linda tried her best with her. Under the dire circumstances when everyone was feeling the tension, Ryan had come up trumps. He organised people, food and dogs so the evening ran as smoothly as possible.

Working into the night I posted my article as soon as it was finished to the newspaper. As usual I sent it to the internal site for the approval of the editorial team. I admit it wasn't my best, but I had been allocated a lemon.

How could one of the senior team believe this was worth investigating. It would work if there had been an inflow of new evidence but there was none. Two outstanding issues remained. The motivation of the victim for being present regularly in the graveyard, while homeless but not drunk was a mystery. The motivation for the assailant to attack him was also unknown.

Dad had faith in the detective in charge of the case and I could perceive no reason to doubt his judgement. He had investigated and identified the circumstances whereby one person had stabbed another to death, but he had established no salient facts in the background of each to sway his judgement.

It was murder. I couldn't disagree although I wanted to write a good story and reveal how badly the young woman in prison had been treated. In the end I could find no justification so used my journalistic expertise to fill the space.

Although working into the early hours, the black coffee at seven o'clock was destined to give me a focus for the day. Deadlines at the newspaper were frantic. My article was due in by noon, but I had posted it ten hours ahead of schedule as I had nothing else to say.

Sitting in the kitchen I scribble some notes for the day ahead.

Check the people in the house are not left on their own. At least two together at any one time. Is that feasible? I can work out the logistics later when we chat.

Return to the boat and fetch Jasmine's laptop and phone.

Revise the article later today as it will be returned by the editorial team. Keep dad's home tidy although it was reasonable apart from his study and train set room.

Satisfied with my ideas I must now wait for the occupants of the house to surface to put my plans into action.

As I sip my second cup of coffee the house remains eerily quiet. No one wants to leave their safe warm beds and face the day. Who can blame them. Lost in thought my phone beeps indicating a text. The message is succinct but insistent. I need to be at the newspaper's office as soon as possible. I groan, but it is the usual editorial panic over a major article. I will have to sit there and rewrite according to their suggestions. The panic is normal and I cannot become focused on it. I will do the changes they suggest but it will still be a crap article.

Before leaving the house, I place a message on the kitchen table so that no one will worry about my disappearance. I also leave my scribbled notes for their perusal.

Arriving in the open plan office area, I drift to the editorial team gathered together in one corner of the large expanse. 'Hi, guys. You wanted me.'

With their usual lack of courtesy no one glances away from the screens. The nearest one points but does not lift his eyes from his task. 'Toby wants to see you.'

'Thank you, guys. And good morning to you as well.'

With no enthusiasm I stroll across to the enclosed frosted glass office. Waiting for Toby is always a pain. He never abides by appointments and deals with staff when he has reached that level of his priority list.

I knock.

'Who is it?'

'Amanda.'

'Come.'

It is unusual for him to respond so quickly as we approach deadline time, so I enter. As he is on the phone, I dump myself on the chair in front of his desk.

Although on the phone and listening while barking the odd words his eyes scrutinise me. He sneers, but I cannot tell whether that is directed at me or the person on the phone. Finishing his call with a goodbye, he plonks his phone on his desk, but the searching stare levelled at me does not diminish.

'The article you wrote about the miscarriage of justice is rubbish. You don't expect me to go with such trite writing, do you?'

It is his usual sounding off. When he has finished his initial rant, he will settle to a discussion of what he wants. Irritated at being called into the office to hear his criticism and wanting to leave as important matters at dad's house need my attention, I sit silent.

'The standard of your work has declined this year.'

The words rile me. The miscarriage of justice article is only a filler and he should understand that was how I approached it. Doesn't he remember that I have completed good and compelling reading earlier in the year and a major article brought many plaudits from those in the office. His view is not true.

Attempting to stand up for myself I want to remind

him about my successes. 'My work has not declined. It has been good. I've completed some outstanding articles, and you know it. Okay, I accept that this piece is not my best but don't blame me.'

He sneers and in a lilting voice he uses for sarcastic remarks, 'Then who should I blame?'

'The person who was too lazy to adopt a considered view. It's not a bloody miscarriage of justice and a read of the crucial part of the evidence would have shown the police and prosecution case to be sound.

'No, I not having it, Amanda. You are trying to blame someone else for your lazy investigation.' I went to speak but he held up his hand. 'Your conclusion that the real issues were the mystery of the murderer and the victim, is lazy rubbish.'

Jumping from my seat, 'Don't bloody run with the article then. Tell the person on your editorial team to write about a miscarriage of justice and then get the bloody paper sued.'

Toby jumps from his seat but stays behind his desk. 'You are getting above your station trying to tell me what to do and blaming others who are not at fault. Get out. You are sacked.'

The words hit me. He has never taken that course of action before. He normally gives me a detailed instruction of how the article needs to be amended. Now is not a good time to lose my job but I will not plead. I am above that.

'Get out. You're sacked.' He turns red in the face and points. He screams it again. 'You're sacked.'

'You can stuff your bloody newspaper. I'm out of here.'

Striding from his office, I slam the door as he continues to yell. The shouting and screaming have focused all those in the outer office, who watch as I run across the open plan area and furiously press the lift button. Barging in as people come out, the tears flow unchecked down my cheeks.

37

Storming through the streets, tears stream across my cheeks and I mutter to myself. In my view the dismissal is unfair and I allow my views on the matter to pour forth as I stride along the London streets. As my temper gradually recedes, I take notice of my surroundings. I pause as my eyes follow the assortment of boats on the River Thames. Studying their progress my breathing slows and I mop up my tears. I settle on a bench and focus on regaining a sense of equilibrium. Being dismissed from my job is irritating especially as I consider it to be unjustified but there will be other job opportunities in the future. It is not the end of the world. Remaining calm is essential for my family's sake. They are far more important than any job. Thinking about them puts everything into perspective. My histrionics are over. Did I regret them? No, but the sacking has put me in an invidious position.

Shall I ring Toby and ask for a meeting? Is a discussion worthwhile at a later date when we have both calmed? He will expect the action to be with me. I am not inclined to ring him. When the reality of not having a job sinks in either tomorrow or the following day will I reconsider?

No. A new era in my life is approaching. No husband. No job. And if the police finally decide on the nature of Jasmine's death, I might be a murder suspect. Also, someone wants to intimidate me and those closest to me, but I do not know who or the reason. Will getting my job back help me?

No. A new and different life beckons. I have enough money in my savings account, providing I keep it away from Jason's grasping hands, to last for several years without needing to work. I won't rush in making the necessary decisions which would include where to live.

A coffee and a slice of cake appeals to me. It will allow me to ring the hospital and enquire about dad's progress. As I am near London Bridge, I stroll along the Embankment searching for a suitable coffee shop.

My phone rings. Strange. Samantha – *Green Boat* shows

on to the screen from my contact list. She has never rung me before. We exchanged numbers when we first met but there has been no phone contact since then.

'Hi, Samantha.' I keep my voice relaxed and chatty.

'These recent developments that have occurred near our boats are worrying. Can we talk? It is urgent?'

I do not wish a lengthy discussion with her as it would be likely to create a disagreement.

'It is important and urgent.' Her insistent voice breaks through my thoughts.

A silent groan escapes. I cannot muster up a feasible excuse. However, there is always the possibility that she might know something to help solve the hassle which surrounds me and my family.

'Okay, tonight at the boats.'

'No. It is more urgent. Where are you? I will come to you.'

'But you are at work.'

'I can grab a few hours out without difficulty.'

There is no avoiding the meeting so I will agree and deal with her urgency which is annoying.

'I'm near Tower Bridge.'

'That's easy, I'm in the City so I will meet you outside the Tower Hotel on the embankment by the Girl with the Dolphin statue.'

'Yes. I know it.'

No further information is given as the phone disconnects. What does she want?

As I stroll towards the appointed meeting place I ponder about Samantha and Montgomery. They are a strange couple. They rarely socialise and when they do all they talk about are green issues and how we must all do our bit to save the planet. Montgomery's dalliance with Jasmine had been an interesting revelation when Samantha had visited me on the boat. As she works in the city, I have the impression that she considers herself superior to the other boat owners.

Confident, well-groomed and attractive sum her up, but her manner can be confrontational if she doesn't get her own way.

I arrive before her and lean with my back against the railings watching the fountain. Samantha appears striding towards me in a smart black top and trousers with a full length leather coat flapping as she walks. I guess the coat will be vegan leather, but I will not comment as I do not wish to receive a lecture on endangered species.

Turning, I allow my eyes to wander over the Thames to the south bank as people walk down to the pier to catch a pleasure boat. This is a meeting I do not need. Hopefully it will be brief and I can return to dad's house and be with the rest of my family. Their safety is uppermost in my mind.

Samantha joins me and adopts the same position, leaning on the railings gazing out over the Thames.

I will wait for her to speak. Perhaps I was rude not to greet her, but there again she ignored my presence when she arrived.

'The police have arrested Montgomery.' She blurts out the words but doesn't turn to face me.

I don't allow the surprise to register on my face. Although she will not have noticed as we are both staring out over the blustery grey waters of the incoming tide. Montgomery had followed me to the churchyard, that put him in the frame for nefarious activities so perhaps the police have discovered something similar. I'm not sympathetic to his predicament. I have always found him arrogant and self-opinionated.

'Why did you tell the police that Montgomery had an affair with Jasmine?' Her voice is harsh and accusatory.

'I didn't.'

'Don't lie, Amanda.' Her lips curl as she sneers with icy contempt. 'You are the only person on the boats that I told. Montgomery and I would not tell the police, so it must have been you.' She pauses and her eyes narrow. 'You are a bitch!' A swift shadow of anger crosses her face as her voice cracks hysterically.

What shall I do now? More hassle coming in my direction. But although she is annoying me, I manage to keep my anger under control. Losing it twice in the same morning is unacceptable.

With a calmness I do not feel I attempt to keep my voice neutral, 'I did not tell the police. Have you considered other possibilities or are you intent on being aggressive to me?'

'There are no other possibilities.' She screams the words at the top of her voice.

Letting out a long sigh, my lips thin with displeasure. What a dreadful woman. It's obvious that she wants to vent her anger on me but is not prepared to listen to my point of view. Keeping calm, I try once again to reason with her. 'There are two people in an affair. Jasmine could have told Benjamin. The police have questioned him extensively and it is the type of information that they will always follow up.'

My statement registers on her face. It is clear that she has not thought of that possibility.

Shaking her head, 'Don't try to squirm out of it. You are the cause of the tension between the boats and the prolonged police investigation.'

The bad few days creep up on me. Why do I have to deal with this intolerable woman? 'Before you continue to throw accusations at me. The only reason I can determine is that you want to deflect attention away from your lifestyle which is so obviously false.' Why had I blurted that out? Whilst I had gained an impression that they lived their lives as a lie I had no proof and had not even explored the possibility that my unfounded supposition could be the truth.

This time Samantha could not keep the surprise from her face as her eyes open wide and her chin drops.

Taking a deep breath before she can respond. 'Why did Montgomery follow me to the graveyard?'

'He would not have done. You must have imagined it and want to blame him.'

'He did. Did he push me into the canal the same afternoon? And why are you trying to defend him?' Puzzlement crosses her face. 'You told me when we had a heart to heart about Montgomery's affair with Jasmine, that you only stayed together because of the sponsorship deal. It strikes me as highly unlikely that you would be defending a man you were only associated with through a convenience of sponsorship. The passion you have for him means you have been lying to me and no doubt putting Montgomery up to following me and pushing me into the canal.'

Amazed at my own lack of tack, I do not see her hand coming. It crashes hard against my face. 'You bitch. I hope you bloody drown in the canal.'

I stagger and grab the handrail. The enormity of her words register along with the implications. She pales but this does not curb her aggression. Taking an attempted second swipe I raise my arm and block the slap. With a scream of frustration, she turns and sprints away.

A few people stop and stare. I ignore them and return to my position of gazing over the Thames as the rain falls. The enormity of my accusatory words cause my legs to weaken. Both Montgomery and Samantha have a motive for murdering Jasmine because of the affair. Perhaps it was both of them. If the murderer comes from *Green World,* then I have put my life on the line.

38

Shaking I continue to clutch at the handrail overlooking the Thames. My temper had got the better of me this morning and it heralded more trouble in the future. I try to calm down and assure myself that Montgomery and Samantha are not the murderers. After my outburst with Samantha, the pair will never speak to me again but that is the least of my concerns.

Jasmine's laptop and phone come to mind. If I am going to solve the issues surrounding me then the laptop and phone might hold the key. I'd had a brief look through it which revealed some information, but I need time to study the different elements and extract all the relevant details. My phone beeps. A text message from Linda. Her and Abigail are meeting dad late this afternoon when he will be discharged. That gives me time to return to the boat and pick up the laptop and phone.

After this morning's debacle with Samantha, the boat is not a sensible place to stay as I do not want another confrontation with her or Montgomery. If I am there, then the person who cut the ropes the other night might be around. With the laptop and phone, I intend to settle myself in a quiet corner of a coffee shop for an hour and sift through the details and download any relevant information.

During the taxi ride from the Tower to Regent Canal my mind revisits the scene of my sacking, but it raises a relevant question for me which I struggle with but will return to later. In my non-existent miscarriage of justice report my only conclusion were the mysteries surrounding the victim and the murderer. Neither had come out. I will apply this idea to Jasmine's death. The laptop and phone might reveal the details about the victim, Jasmine. Later I will try to put together a profile of the possible person involved given that the motivation of the crime will be deeply hidden. I am convinced it is a crime and not accidental.

The taxi drops me at the northern end of Regents Park and I follow the usual route along the towpath. As the path twists to give a distant view of the boats, a police car with blue flashing lights inches its way along the towpath and parks close to the boats. I hurry forward. My phone rings but I ignore it as I wish to discover why the police are here.

Several police mill around on the towpath. Closing in, one is standing on my boat. What's he doing? I increase my pace with nervous apprehension coursing through me. One officer points in my direction and Constable Smith steps up from the boat to the towpath and waits for me to join him.

'What's happened?'

'I've just tried to ring you as I only arrived at the scene a few minutes ago. Your boat has been broken into.'

My heart sinks. How many more incidents will be directed at me? 'When? Is there much damage?'

'I don't know as I've only just arrived and the first report only mentioned the damage to the entrance door and locks. Do you feel brave and want to have a look? Or shall I check first and report back, it might help to ease the shock.'

'I'll come.'

The officers stand out of the way as Constable Smith leads me down the steps into the boat. I brace myself expecting to be greeted by a scene of devastation. He looks around. 'Nothing here that I can see. No wanton damage. Shall we check the rest of the boat?'

I blink in agreement. Nothing has been disturbed. Words fail me. This is not turning out to be a good day. There is no damage in the dining area or galley. He reaches the bow.

'Is anything out of place. Where do you keep money and credit cards?'

'Money and cards I carry in my handbag and do not leave them unattended on the boat. The small number of documents that are not on line are in here.' I open a small locker under the main bed. 'The same as usual.'

'Perhaps the thief was disturbed or it is more of the hassle that you have been suffering recently.'

At least he has conceded that I have been on the receiving end of several episodes intended to intimidate me. 'Wait, there is one more place to check.' I move to the front cupboard under the stairs and open it. Empty.

'I can tell from your face that you expected to find something. What is missing?'

'You'd better sit, so I can explain.'

He tilts his head to one side, drops onto a chair and focuses on me.

'Benjamin moved to his flat from *Carpe Diem* as soon as you permitted.' He nods. 'I visited him and he asked me to sort out Jasmine's clothes and belongings and to check the boat after the cleaners had visited.'

'Jasmine's belongings?'

'I bagged the clothes ready for a charity.'

'Did you find any belongings?'

'No, not then. Odd bits of paper mainly receipts from a coffee shop. Trivia. But when I checked his boat, I found a laptop and phone hidden at the back of one of the storage areas. The black bags of her clothes plus the computer and phone were stored in that cupboard.' I point towards the empty space under the stairs.

'Did you look at them?'

I gulp as this could be tricky in case the police discover them as they will have my fingerprints on them.'

I didn't know whether they were broken so I opened them but both had a password and appeared operational. I left them in the cupboard expecting to return them to Benjamin.

'Did anyone else know that you were inspecting Benjamin's boat or that you had found the items?'

'I told no one about the tasks. Benjamin knew, but I did the check in full daylight so anyone could have noticed me go on or leave *Carpe Diem*.'

39

Despite a few quizzical looks from Constable Smith, he accepts my story, which is such a relief. The door is easily repaired from the leverage damage. A friendly policeman comes to the rescue and secures it, but it could easily be opened again with a crowbar, the tool probably used by those that had broken in. As it is now mid-afternoon I am desperate to be at dad's house when he returns from hospital. His face will show me whether he has recovered.

The police are checking with the neighbouring boats, which is the second time recently, as they visited each boat after the ropes on *Serendipity* had been cut. The neighbours will not be pleased as they are being drawn into a matter that does not concern them. But was the death of Jasmine, and the subsequent hassle of me, caused by one of the boat residents? It is easy to observe from any of the boats what happens. Someone could be watching and waiting. Samantha is top of my list after the aggression she had shown me earlier today.

A text from Linda informs me dad's discharge has been held up by the administrative matters of obtaining the necessary painkillers from the overworked hospital pharmacy and that he is walking and feeling fine. While assured by the information, I worry about him. The unbuttoned cardigan springs to mind. Will he cope after being attacked?

With the boat temporarily locked and as the police officers leave, I glance at the other boats and particularly *Green World* but there is no evidence to suggest that the residents are on board. I try to convince myself that the complete absence of movement is normal. Samantha is at work and also Montgomery. *Green World* will be quiet throughout the day. *Carpe Diem* no longer has residents as Benjamin has moved to his new flat. *Kingfisher* appears quiet, but it often did. Letitia might be painting in the bow or on location. Russell is a rare visitor. The tranquil nature of the boats has me worried as much as if they had been busy.

Snapping out of my mind delving into the mysterious

depths I resolve to keep an even perspective. Not everyone is plotting against me. The world doesn't have a down on me. It is one person. The rest are fine and only wish to carry on with their lives without my life impacting on them and the police interference.

Looking back at the closed and temporarily sealed *Serendipity,* I pause. It has been a key part of life for the past few years, but it is time to settle the issues and move on. It might be time to leave *Serendipity* and relocate. It's a sad thought but I have no friends to leave behind.

Time is no longer crucial as dad has not left the hospital yet, so I will walk and try to clear my thoughts. The rain teams down from a leaden sky. Not dressed appropriately is the least of my problems. Water trickles icily down my neck despite flicking up my collar. The overcast sky merging into the fog will last all day, but the walk to dad's house might help me rationalise recent events.

Under the tree canopy is dark and the only sound is the hammering of rain on the trees which overhang the path. I miss having Rufus by my side but he is already installed at dad's house. The inclement weather has cleared the towpath of the normal walkers, joggers and tourists. A sudden movement makes me jump. Jason steps out of the gloom from behind a nearby tree. 'What are you doing hiding behind a tree?'

'Waiting for you.' He steps closer and despite the rain his breath reeks of alcohol. 'I need money.' His voice is harsh and he gives me a look of withering contempt.

I have to shake my head in disbelief. Jason has been waiting to ambush me and demand money. 'No chance. You have had all the money I am prepared to give you.'

He winces in annoyance and the line of his mouth tightens a fraction more, 'But I'm in a mess and need help.'

There is no denying it. His clothes, never the best or stylish are dirty with grease and other substances smeared down the front. His overall appearance, unshaven and hair uncombed, is the image of a street sleeper. 'You had your chance, Jason and blew it.'

He takes a step closer, 'Give me what's in your purse. You always carry plenty of cash.'

'No way, Jason. Get a job and a life. I will not have you expecting me to give you handouts.'

He snarls as the heavens open and he steps even closer, grabbing my arm, 'I want money.'

I return the snarl. Staring up to him with icy disapproval, 'Does the name Jason Agnew ring a bell with you. You have been stealing from my bank account for years. Well, I've put a stop to it.'

He wrenches my arm, which hurts, and leans his face close to mine. His foul-smelling alcohol breath engulfs me making me gag. 'I know you have stopped the account, but I can't live without money.'

'Get a bloody job like the rest of us.' Before I can move away, he twists my arm in a vicious manner, making my muscles scream in agony. 'Ahh! Get off me.' I struggle to free myself, battering and shoving him but he is too strong. 'I'll scream.'

Drawing in a deep breath his other hand slaps me across the face with such force that I lose my balance and stumble into the tree. He raises his hand again. I cower expecting another attack. Snatching my bag from my arm, he flicks it open and grabs my purse.

'No.' I moan dismally. The hand crashes against my head again.

Blackness whirls around me as a strange roaring sound fills my ears. I am completely vulnerable as my strength has gone. My whole body trembles and my legs turn to jelly. Grasping the tree for support I sway, but keep my footing. Much to my relief he staggers away and disappears over the bridge in the rain and mist clutching my purse.

40

The rain eases as I gather my thoughts after the attack by Jason. He is in desperate need of help but I will not be the one to assist him. Perhaps Linda will be able to communicate with him. Stopping in a bus shelter, I remove the compact from my bag. Jason has stolen the purse. About one hundred pounds in cash and nothing else apart from receipts. My face is blotchy and the cut above my eye dribbles blood.

The second hit from Jason had landed on my head. Twisting to the light the left side of my face is swollen. Both he and Samantha had caught me on the same side of my face and I will have a black eye as the bruise develops.

Cold, wet and shivering I patch my face the best I can. The weakness from my legs after the attack by Jason has dissipated. Setting off at a striding pace I only have half a mile to travel.

Opening the door, I call out and hear the voice I want. Dad is home. Turning into the lounge I rush across and hug him. His pale and drawn face manages a smile, 'It's good to be home.'

'Where are the others?'

'Linda is in the kitchen, cleaning and tidying, and the youngsters have gone shopping but will be back soon. What have you done to your face?'

I want to avoid a conversation with dad about what had happened until I can work out the best way of framing the events to cause him less stress.

The front doorbell rings. Linda calls out and her footsteps sound in the hall as she goes to answer the summons. The voices are too indistinct. Linda comes into the lounge followed by Constable Smith and a woman police constable in uniform.

Constable Smith crosses to dad, 'I'm glad you are out of hospital, sir. And I am sorry, but you will appreciate it is my duty.'

Dad has a resigned look although I am confused by his

statement.

Constable Smith faces me. 'You do not have to say anything. But, it may harm your defence if you do not mention when questioned something which you later rely on in court. Anything you do say may be given in evidence. I am arresting you in connection with the suspicious death of Jasmine Ruth.'

Dad rubs his chin as I slump into a seat because my legs will no longer support me. The uniformed constable moves to stand next to me.

With a strangely preoccupied frown dad raises his eyes, 'Constable, I do not know whether you will answer, but has the death of Jasmine been confirmed as murder.'

Constable Smith looks at me and then again at dad. 'Yes, sir. The Home Office pathologist is convinced it is a deliberate death.'

'Thank you.' My eyes open wide as I stare frantically at dad.

'Don't worry, Amanda. The current collection of evidence points to you. As you did not kill Jasmine you have nothing to fear from the police process. But tell the Constable the whole truth even if it looks black for you.'

'Yes, dad.' I stand, 'Let's get on with it.'

41

It has reached early evening before my arrest has been processed and they have fed me. I was too stressed to be hungry, but they insisted as I had revealed that I had not eaten all day. They offered to delay questioning until tomorrow but that involved spending the night in a police cell. It was not something that appealed, to put it mildly, and I intended to avoid it if possible. So, I declined and asked to be questioned as soon as possible.

Sitting alone in the interview room where I have been placed, my thoughts spiral. My recent life has gradually been collapsing but today it has fallen into a gigantic dark hole. It has not been a good day. Now all I can do is to follow dad's advice.

The door opens. Inula strides in as brightly coloured as when we met before. Today her ensemble is turquoise and bright orange. A half smile of greeting flits across her face and she drops on to the seat next to me. 'You have been arrested and they expect to charge you with murder after this evening's questioning. Do you understand?'

'Yes, thank you, Inula. I realise the seriousness of the situation and have come to terms with the ridiculous notion that the police think I killed her. But this evening I intend to remain calm and answer their questions.'

The door opens and Constable Smith enters and in a precise manner closes it behind him. He acknowledges my presence with a tight-lipped smile, then sits and completes the formalities with the recording machine.

'Before we review the party again, I wish to ask you questions about other matters.'

I am focused. Despite the day I've had I will not lose my temper. 'Yes, please do.'

Forcing myself to be calm, I resolve to demonstrate a polite and helpful attitude throughout the interview. It might be a struggle but it's what dad would expect.

'When you were brought to the police station under

arrest the Duty Sergeant noticed a laceration and bruising on your face. At his request a doctor examined you.'

This would be slow and pedantic, but I had no option but to stick with it.

'Can I ask you for the benefit of the tape whether you feel medically okay and are prepared to answer questions.'

'Yes, I am comfortable and have no issues with my slight injuries.'

'As there have been other incidents associated with you, can you tell me how you obtained the laceration above your eye and bruising to your face? Could you also provide an account of your movements for earlier today? Apart from the time you were with me.'

Inula purses her lips.

Forcing myself to relax, I raise my chin and stare intently at his face, 'I've not had a good day. Early this morning at nine o'clock I attended the newspaper office on the South Bank and was fired from my job.'

The Constable's eyes focus, 'Was it expected?'

'No. It was on impulse from the editor when he lost his temper.'

'Do you still have a major article coming out this week, the one which you received the death threat about.'

Inula shuffles in her seat, 'Constable, is this linked to the current questioning. I am unclear about the death threat.'

I do not want my solicitor, as good as she is to keep interfering.

'It is okay. The death threat was sent to the paper and the police have investigated but no one as far as I know has been arrested.'

The Constable rolls his shoulders. 'There have been no arrests.'

'I do not know whether the editor will go with the article that I wrote. As it contains virtually no new information it would be my expectation that it will be canned. The deadline for reporting is three days before publication although the article I wrote was submitted early.'

'Please carry on.'

'After I left the newspaper, I received a call from Samantha who lives on *Green World*.'

'Yes, I know the lady.'

'We met near Tower Bridge when she accused me of giving the police personal information about her and Montgomery.'

'What was the personal information?'

'Montgomery had an affair with Jasmine. I did not tell the police. Samantha and I did not agree and when I accused her of lying, she hit me.'

He frowns in confusion but makes no comment.

'I then met you at the break-in at the boat, when I didn't tell you the whole truth.'

Inula touches my hand, 'I would recommend that you say no more until we prepare a formal statement.'

'Thanks for the advice but I wish to continue. Is that okay with you. Constable?'

He nods in agreement and flaps his hand for me to resume.

This interview is stressing me out, but I must keep calm.

I breathe deeply for a few moments to steady myself. 'It's about Jasmine's laptop that I found hidden away in a cupboard. I did get past the first screen.'

His eyes widen with interest and he leans forward, 'What did you find?

'I was pressed for time. Various drafts of Benjamin's novels. An account number and sort code for Jasmine Enterprises.'

'Can you remember them?'

'No.'

'A list of folders each named after the people on the boats.'

'Did you check yours?'

'Yes, it was empty.'

'Did you check others?'

'No. I didn't have time.'

'What about the phone?'

'The front screen showed bank access, the numbers for which were in a directory on the laptop.'

Inula gives a small cough to attract my attention, 'Be wary, you may be about to admit an illegal act.'

I appreciate her concern and reach across to give her arm a reassuring squeeze, 'Thanks for the warning. I accessed the account and found it contained over a quarter of a million pounds.'

Even the constable couldn't maintain a dead pan expression and he raises his eyebrows.

'At that point my daughter arrived, and I closed the phone and laptop and placed them in the cupboard from where they were stolen.'

'Are you okay to carry on?'

'Yes. After I left you. It began to rain heavily. In the wooded section of the towpath, I met my husband. We had an argument. He hit me twice, causing the laceration and stole my purse.' I thought about whether I should implicate him long and hard during the arrest process but could think of no reason to ignore an attack on me.

The Constable stops the tape. 'Mrs Mallory and Mrs Pettigrew. You will be aware that this interview has given the police information that must be checked.'

'Can I ask about charges as various possible offences have been mentioned?'

'Too soon to say I'm afraid. Senior officers must be consulted. The laptop and phone have been stolen but the other issues can be verified by the police which we will do, although I expect them to be confirmed.'

The door opens and another Constable enters and passes Constable Smith a note. He reads it. 'This is a further complication in this case. And it is not good news for you Mrs Mallory. This was sent to the editor. Please can you read it and offer any comments.'

It is a pity your reporter didn't drown when she fell into the canal.

Inula catches my hand. We both shake our heads.

Day Seven

42

Staring at the police bail documents on the kitchen table, I sip my first morning black coffee as the early shimmers of the gloomy daylight reach the room along with the pounding of the rain. The weather suits my mood. Yesterday's disastrous events have left me in a state of despondency and agitation. First of all, I was sacked. Then came the assault by Samantha. After that the discovery of the break in on the boat. Then Jason's attack on me and then finally my arrest and questioning. The events have impacted on me and a cloud of gloom has settled over me. What will happen next is at the forefront of my mind.

I had been released on bail because of the information I had provided. One factor must have been more important than the others, but I couldn't decide which had gripped Constable Smith's attention. The flash of his eyes when I explained about the argument with Samantha and Montgomery's affair with Jasmine, stood out for me, but I could not be certain.

How long before they come for me again? Perhaps a day or two. An icy shiver travels through my body at the thought. They will check out the information I had given them but would dismiss most of it and then return their attention to me. Shuffling sounds from upstairs reach me, which suggests the others are rising from their slumbers. Dad drifts into the kitchen.

'Dad, how are you? Should you be up? Go back to bed and I will bring you a cup of tea.'

A look of veiled amusement crosses his face and he grins, 'I'm fine and do not need to be in bed. My head is clear and the bruises ache but nothing to trouble me or to worry about painkillers.'

I pop the kettle on.

'We need to talk, Amanda. You are caught up in Jasmine's case which will take a long time. You could be in custody.'

That is not an inspiring thought. Images of me incarcerated in prison flash through my mind as I shake uncontrollably. I busy myself making tea and hope that dad does not notice.

After a pause he continues, 'The police process is slow and pedantic. It might take months after they charge you. A prime suspect is identified, in this case it is you, but the time is spent building a case and proving beyond reasonable doubt that you committed the crime. With one key fact they may well arrest and charge you and keep you in custody.'

'Dad that's terrifying.' My heart races and I have this urge to run away and hide.

'It is, because I do not want my daughter holed up in jail for four or five months before they release you.' He sips his tea and grins at me in a reassuring manner. 'Last night you provided them with information. Keep telling the truth however bad it seems. I expected you to be in custody for two or three weeks.'

I open my eyes in terror. He pats my hand and looks at his empty mug.

Unable to resist a smile, I jump up and make him another cup of tea.

'Is there anything I can do which will help me stay out of jail.'

I place a new cup of tea for him on the table and a black coffee for me. My brain needs to be alert.

'Yes, there is, I've a plan.'

My eyes open wide. He is poorly and continually looks dishevelled but there appears little wrong with his mind. I hope dad can remove the nightmare into which I have descended.

Rubbing his chin in his usual thoughtful pose. 'There is the victim and killer. The background of each tells the reason for the crime.' He screws up his face. 'Did you get anywhere with Jack's case about the murder in the churchyard?'

How he suddenly changes tact confuses me, but I will go with him. 'No, there appeared little doubt about the act of her stabbing him but there was a considerable mystery about both the victim and the young woman who murdered him.'

'An unusual case which is rare. Going to court without the background information on the victim or killer would normally be dismissed.'

'Dad, we are supposed to be talking about me.'

'Different case, same principles. They will have no witnesses to Jasmine's death.'

'Is it definitely murder as they took a long time to decide?'

'I mentioned before that the pathologist was slow and pedantic but rarely wrong. They would have called in a Home Office pathologist. While they might have made a technical breach in procedures it is highly unlikely. If they conclude murder, there is little doubt.'

He has another sip of his tea. 'It is nearly eight o'clock and I told the others we would plan over breakfast. Bacon rolls all round, and we will have an extra visitor who eats like a horse.'

43

It is the strangest breakfast meeting I have ever attended. Dad's expression is bright and cheerful although his appearance is a little dishevelled. His jumper is threadbare and his hair stands on end. He munches enthusiastically on his bacon bap as he studies the others sitting around the kitchen table.

Linda sits next to him in a beautifully embroidered dressing gown with a bowl of fruit, yogurt and muesli. Abigail attempting to appear wide eyed and force herself awake, follows her grandad's choice of breakfast with a bacon bap. The two men, Ryan and Freddie sit at the end of the table with plates full of everything that was in the fridge suitable for breakfast. Freddie as tall as Ryan but twice as broad needs two seats but he copes with one. A strange meeting.

Dad opens his hand to Freddie, 'We worked together for years.'

'We did that!' Freddie guffaws as he spears another piece of black pudding.

Dad's mouth twitches with amusement, 'We meet regularly now as Freddie is the master engineer for the train sets.'

Ryan lifts his head and drops his fork with a clatter. The excitement registers on his face, 'You have a trainset, can I see it?'

'Yes, of course. It's upstairs.'

'Dad, dad!' I tap the table with my forefinger to attract his attention, 'This is a planning meeting.'

'So it is.' He pats the back of my hand. 'Don't worry. Us normal mortals do not rush around like journalists.' He turns to Freddie, 'Shall we show young Ryan the train set later?'

'Definitely, boss, but Amanda and Linda are becoming agitated and poor Abigail has not yet joined the real world this morning.'

A cheerful friendly man, who despite his size and eating power is acutely observant of the people who have been thrown together.

Dad looks around the table. 'All settled?' We nod. 'The police will search for background information about the victim and murderer. Our investigations, the same as with the police, will be conducted with support. No one will be exposed to danger and we will be in constant contact with each other. We know the victim, but we need a detailed background search. We will also draw up a list of possible suspects and methodically investigate them.'

Shaking my head. The plan is a pipe dream as there is no way we can follow it. We are just a group of ordinary individuals who do not have the backup or information that the police have at their fingertips.

Dad grins, 'Amanda you are in charge, tell us what we need to do.'

I focus on him. Has he lost it completely? A long silence follows when everyone stares expectantly at me. The connections gradually materialise as this is no different to my former role on the newspaper. 'As an investigative journalist.' I pause, grin and study those around the table.

Dad smiles and nods. As my thought processes come together, I elaborate, 'The police and investigative journalists do their job in different ways to achieve the same result. The police have manpower and information whereas an investigative journalist relies heavily on hearsay.'

Linda listens attentively but her face is etched with worry, 'It's a brilliant idea but I wonder about safety.'

Dad reaches across and pats her reassuringly on the arm, 'There are always two of three of us close by, Freddie, you explain.'

He opens the large black bag that is positioned by his chair and pulls out cables and earpieces which he places on the table. 'These are the tools we require. It will ensure we are protected and that everything is recorded. Someone will always be nearby. I expect it will often be me or Ryan. No one can dismiss us easily.'

Linda shuffles in her seat. It's important to hear her views. 'Linda, do you have reservations?'

'None at all. A brilliant plan. I'm in.'

Dad grins and rubs his hands together in an enthusiastic manner.

44

Dad is a genius to have thought up such a plan. It's essential to carry out a non-controversial test to check that the equipment performs correctly. I choose to approach Letitia as she appears the least involved. Abigail and Ryan will be on *Serendipity*. Dad and Linda intend to walk the dogs nearby, while Freddie will sit on various benches along the canal as though a tourist. In his rucksack, he has all the recording equipment.

Initially it might be tricky as I have never been wired up for an interview where several other people can hear the conversation. Planning with the likes of dad and Freddie gives me confidence. If we lose contact as we are unfamiliar with the technology or if it fails then Abigail and Ryan will come to *Kingfisher* searching for me.

Approaching the back door of the *Kingfisher* from the stern deck, it is wide open. I rap hard, 'Letitia, Russell are you there.' I hope he is away as I'm not in the mood to deal with his advances.

After a few moments delay, 'Hi, Amanda, come in. I'm painting in the front lounge.' It is the same route that I followed when visiting before to help her clear up the brushes.

'I've just finished a session so let's sit and chat, there has been a lot going on locally and as usual I'm not up to speed.'

It is the perfect opportunity, but it is a strange realisation that I have five people listening.

'Is there any reason you have come?'

'Only because we are neighbours. *Serendipity* was cast adrift deliberately and then the break in occurred. I thought I would check as you mentioned previously that some of your paintings had been stolen.'

'You are kind to be concerned after the turmoil you must have experienced. However, I'm relaxed as my paintings are selling well and as I told you before, we are leaving. Russell has already left and I will join him in the near future, but there are a few paintings of local scenes that I wish to complete first.

I smile as their exquisite boat contains a chiming clock. The Westminster Chime sounded noon.

'A few more days and I shall leave the boat, have a holiday abroad and return to a new location.'

I am conscious this is only a test for the technology but for once Letitia desires to chat so I will oblige her. 'Do you paint when you are abroad?'

'No, far too complicated to carry everything through customs. Also, foreign landscapes are not my style. I stick with my strengths, English scenery.' She laughs. 'You told me when we first met you dabbled in painting.'

I raise my eyebrows in amusement, 'Dabble is the right word but I enjoy it although I have never produced a full painting.'

Letitia relaxes back in her seat as the autumn sun beats down through the sunroof of the lounge. 'I have finished for the day as the light will not be right this afternoon and I am partial to a gin and tonic before lunch, will you join me?'

My inclination is to decline but I might discover her opinion about Jasmine's paintings, which are a mystery to me, the same as the woman. 'I'm with you, Letitia, as I desire nothing more than to relax after the recent traumas.'

She disappears to the galley to fix the drinks.

The slightest of plan forms in my mind. I have no idea how the others will reflect on the ramblings. But dad is right, I can use my experience in investigative journalism. Sometimes it is direct questioning but normally when interviewing people, often surreptitiously, it is open questions that gain results.

Letitia proffers a large gin, with a bottle of tonic on the side, which I accept. 'Do you allow your paintings to be viewed before completion?'

'Yes.' She flips back the muslin screen that she folded over the work on the easel as I arrived.

I am surprised that she will allow me to view it, although I don't have to peer closely, as it is instantly recognisable. 'It's Little Venice along the canal from here.'

'You are quick in recognising the scene. The rest of the painting requires the details of the boats and the people, but I can finish those from anywhere from the photo I took.'

It will be too direct to ask about Jasmine's painting but one of the files on Jasmine's laptop was labelled Suffolk Seascape. It might be worth bringing it into the conversation. I pretend to study the painting of the Little Venice landscape with intense interest, as these thoughts swirl through my mind.

Taking a large sip of gin. I giggle. 'Sorry, but I will get my art history wrong, the style, to my amateur mind, is reminiscent of Constable in Suffolk.'

'First rate. I was born in Dedham, Constable's country, so I favour his style which I learned from local painters and did a great deal of research about the man.'

Taking another large sip of gin to suggest I am relaxed I intend to continue our little chat. Whether the guys on the earpieces agree with my approach will be a different matter. 'I love the coastal walks along the Suffolk Coast.'

Letitia taking another sip of gin, puts her head on one side. 'Have you been there often?'

'Yes, mum and dad would take me on weekend breaks to coastal towns. Despite growing into a truculent teenager, I wanted them to continue and I remember walking the paths on the salt marshes near the sea. The blend of the sky, water and marshes was truly wonderful.'

'Then if you want to develop your painting, fix on that idea and practice until you are satisfied with the outcome.'

'Have you ever painted such scenes, as I would be interested in buying one?'

'No. I have not.' She suddenly stands up. Her friendly expression is no longer evident as she gulps back the remainder of her gin. 'While we could chat all afternoon, I must do the shopping.' I swiftly finish my gin and move towards the exit.

We hug our farewells, but there is no warmth from her.

I step from the boat. I'd enjoyed the chat although she

had terminated the conversation rather abruptly. The result was unexpected as I had told no one what I had viewed on Jasmine's machine.

We have agreed to return to the house in separate ways. I put the kettle on anticipating that everyone will require a drink.

Once we are all settled around the kitchen table, Dad glances at me as he expects me to assume the lead. 'Were the communications okay, could you hear?'

Linda opens her hand to Freddie, 'Brilliant job, I could hear perfectly as Charles and I wandered in Regent's Park.' Dad nods his agreement and smiles.

Ryan pats Freddie on the back. 'Perfect, we could hear every word on *Serendipity*.'

'Freddie how was it from your point of view?'

'Recording was perfect, but you might be interested in the analysis of the conversation although I did not know what the pair of you were talking about.'

I wasn't expecting any useful information as we picked Letitia as a trial for the technology, but her reaction about Suffolk Seascape surprised me.'

'I ran the last part of the conversation through a cheap rate lie detector because her voice changed.'

I had noticed a change as she wanted the conversation to end quickly after appearing relaxed.

'The lie detector showed a big spike when you talked about the Suffolk Seascape.'

'But why would she lie about a painting?' Dad glances at me. 'I'm with you now dad, let's put it on the list for further investigation.'

45

For my second interview of the day, I have chosen Benjamin. Dad has issued a chilling warning that in the eyes of the police Benjamin will be a critical suspect and therefore might be the murderer. I press the buzzer for the flat and wait. How will he greet me?

The door opens and Benjamin with a warm and friendly expression, steps aside to allow me to enter. No hugging this time. Perhaps he has returned to his old non tactile approach. As soon as the door closes, he envelopes me in an embracing hug and gives me two long kisses on the cheek. I'd been wrong. His enthusiastic welcome unnerves me. His breath reeks of alcohol, but there are no empty glasses. The flat is remarkably tidy so where had the alcohol on his breath come from?

'It is so good to see you again, Amanda. I thought about visiting you on *Serendipity* several times in the last couple of days as you had not checked back with me about Jasmine's belongings.'

'I've been involved with the police several times.'

He laughs which is not like the man who lived on the boat next to ours. Most of the time his expression was neutral, almost bordering on moody, and it was rare to hear him laugh. 'Yes, they also keep coming to pester me with daft questions. How they expect me to know details about Jasmine's life I do not know. I keep giving them the same answers, but they still keep trying.'

Leading the way into the lounge he pulls the door down on the drinks' cupboard. Again, no sign of used glasses. All the bottles and glasses are neatly arranged.

'G and T? I enjoyed the chat we had on the day after the party.'

The words used surprise me. I remembered the chat, but he referred to after the party and not after the death of Jasmine. Perhaps it emphasises the convenience of the relationship.

The gin is huge, and he places the bottle of tonic next to it and slumps into the armchair where he reclines in a rather peculiar position. All lopsided and with his legs stuck out at strange angles. From the vagueness of his approach to his chair and the smell on his breath, I conclude he is drunk. I will start with the bad news and consider how he reacts.

'Benjamin.' He grins inanely at me and lifts his glass. I do not detect a man who wants a serious conversation, but as I need one, he has no option. 'I've bad news.' The grin on his face does not disappear but he remains silent.

'I sorted out the black bags of her clothes and belongings. There were no personal effects. An odd lipstick or makeup compact but nothing of value, so I bagged the clothes for the charity shop.' He appears disinterested. 'But I checked the boat as you asked and found a laptop and phone.' It catches his attention and his slowly closing eyelids open wide. 'I assume they belonged to Jasmine.'

'They were not mine. Have you brought them with you?'

'No.' He concentrates and for the first time puts his drink on the coffee table and leans forward resting his elbows on his knees. Although he tries to focus on my face, he has difficulty and keeps adjusting his head backwards and forwards.

'I put them in a cupboard on my boat and popped out for a few hours expecting to come to visit you that evening.'

The grinning face has transformed. His eyes are narrowed and his lips are set into a thin hard line.

'My boat was broken into. When I arrived back the police were already there.'

'Did they steal much and was there significant damage?'

It was a standard comment that reveals he is not interested. Leaning back in his chair he stares at the ceiling but screws up his face to concentrate.

'The intruders did no damage, but I am afraid only stole Jasmine's laptop, phone and clothes.'

Downing the rest of his drink, he does not ask if I need a refill, but picks up my half-finished glass and crosses to the drinks' cabinet. He wants time to think, which I will allow him and not chunter with small talk as I often do.

After topping up the drinks, he turns with a broad smile. Why the change? 'I'm sure Jasmine only used her laptop for trivial matters and to search the web for her painting ideas. Her phone would contain nothing of interest as few people rang her and she initiated few calls. So, thanks for sorting out and I am sorry about the break-in on *Serendipity* but the loss of the items is not a concern as they were meaningless.' He waves his hand to dismiss the conversation.

Then he settles in his chair, 'Sorry Amanda, but I must apologise.'

The change of tone to deeper and more serious comes as a surprise. I wonder whether the others listening in have detected it.

I smile, 'What about?'

'When you mentioned I could obtain the local gossip from Jason.'

'You stated that he would not be invited to your flat.' I open my eyes wide as the truth dawns on me. 'You already knew about him and Jasmine.'

He rubs his eyes and grimaces in wry acknowledgement. 'I had my suspicions for a while, but I needed to finish a book for the publishers, so I was in total concentration the two nights before she died, but I found it difficult to focus and went to find Jasmine to ask her to go to the off-licence for more booze as I anticipated a long overnight session. She would not expect me to break my concentration. She wasn't on *Carpe Diem* so I looked around and saw your boat had lights, so I assumed she had popped over to chat to you. I found her in your galley area making drinks with no clothes on.'

'Thanks for telling me, Benjamin. It came as a shock when Jason told me, but I can understand why you were reticent to inform me.'

One of the principal reasons for wanting to interview him is to discover whether Jasmine had ghosted his novels, but now is not the right time. He needs to be relaxed and not thinking through the implications.

Leaving Benjamin's flat with a sigh of relief I head back to dad's house for a debrief. On the way I stop off at an artisan bakery and buy a large selection of pastries. The shopkeeper laughs and asks if I am feeding an army. It's reassuring to have a normal light-hearted conversation. I know that it's not the whole world that is against me but that just one person is responsible.

Settling ourselves around the table we sip our drinks and munch on the pastries. I'm glad that I bought plenty as Freddie has a good appetite. When the plate is empty, I attempt to refocus everyone's thoughts on the important issues.

Tapping my fingers on the table to grab their attention I launch in with my views. 'I don't think we have gained a great deal more information from Benjamin. I don't know if you picked it up in the recordings but he was very drunk. Crossing the room was problematic for him as he was so unsteady. His greeting was also different and he hugged me rather enthusiastically and the kiss on my cheek was longer than I wanted.'

The others around the table don't comment so I continue, 'The only interesting point was when he referred to events as after the party rather than after Jasmine's death. It strikes me that he is not grieving for her.'

They all nod at my brief synopsis but no one has anything further to add.

46

Dad and Linda take the dogs for an after-lunch walk. They have a regular route which passes the canal boats to check everything is in order with *Serendipity*. They discover a note pinned to the door of the boat from Montgomery and Samantha asking me to contact or visit them but they leave it in place not wishing to bring attention to themselves.

I am wired so that everyone can listen as I approach *Serendipity* and detach the note from the door and pretend to read it in case I am being watched. The rest of the team settle themselves in their allotted positions nearby, but out of site. I presume the meeting will not be friendly. When arrested, I reported to the police that Samantha had hit me. Dad thinks it likely they will have taken Samantha to a police station for questioning, although would be unlikely to charge her as there are no independent witnesses.

I would have been wary to meet up with the troublesome pair without my newly formed backup. Attempting to appear relaxed I approach *Green World* with only a little apprehension as I have the feeling that before long the mystery of Jasmine's death might be solved.

Stepping on to the stern deck, I tap on the door. Montgomery opens it. 'Come in.' The deadpan face does not flicker and there are no thanks for responding to the cursory note they had left. He leaves the door open which is perfect as otherwise I would have met them on the stern deck. I do not intend to be isolated with them.

He leads the way to the front lounge. Samantha sits on one of the long benches and does not stand. Her face remains expressionless. I am not offered a seat, not that I expected one. Neither appear to want to initiate the conversation. 'What do you want, guys?'

'You ratted on me to the police.' Samantha's lips barely move, 'That is the second time it has happened.' She sticks out her lower lip and glowers at me. 'You must have gone to them and reported our conversation.'

I will not be forced on the back foot in this exchange. 'Just for once listen to me, Samantha. You didn't consider my words last time and that caused the issue. I did not tell the police about his,' I pause for emphasis and point directly at Montgomery who stands next to me, 'affair with Jasmine.'

I let a silence develop as I edge slightly away from him as he is too close for comfort.

'Yet again, Samantha, you have got it wrong. You only ever want to believe in the world that surrounds you and make the events and incidents fit into your confused line of thinking, instead of working out what really happened.'

She snarls at me with icy contempt, 'Are you telling me you didn't go to the police because I don't believe you. There is no other way they could have found out.'

I curl my lip as I scan between them. 'On the day you assaulted me I was involved in several incidents. Your bloody-minded and aggressive attitude was just one of them. Why I should tell you what happened I don't know, as it is none of your business, but I will.'

I move further away from Montgomery who stands scowling but not moving. 'My boat was broken into and the police are looking for those responsible and believe it is connected with the people at the party.'

Montgomery flaps his hand in a contemptuous manner, 'It has nothing to do with us.'

I give a false smile, 'But it does as Jasmine's phone and laptop were stolen.'

Both pairs of eyes immediately focus on me. They want to ask questions. It's obvious their minds are ticking over the possible implications for them. Interestingly, they look worried.

'During the early part of that same evening, the police arrested me and took me to the police station for questioning about the murder of Jasmine.'

Samantha flicks her hand, 'You are talking rubbish. It is only a suspicious death; you are exaggerating by referring to it as murder.'

'Look it up on your phone.' I snap back. My patience is wearing thin and I'm struggling to control my irritation. 'It has been confirmed as murder.'

Samantha flicks at her phone, and after reading a screen, lays it down next to her. 'Did the police caution you?' It was the first time that her voice sounded normal. Montgomery raises his eyebrows as he understands the implication of her question.

'Yes. It was a formal arrest after caution, and I was placed in a cell for several hours until the duty solicitor attended. My eye was bleeding, so I was examined by the police doctor.'

Samantha opens her eyes wide, 'I never cut your face. You lying cow.' Her voice rises hysterically on the last three words and her face reddens with fury.

I sneer at them with open resentment, 'As usual, Samantha you do not wait to be aware of all the facts. You hit me in the morning, but my estranged husband hit me in the same place in the afternoon, causing the bleeding.'

'Jason?'

'Correct. He was having an affair with Jasmine. She was a good time girl, wasn't she?' I allow my eyes to rest on Montgomery to emphasise my words.

Samantha stands, 'We want to give you a friendly warning. Leave out any mention of us to the police.'

I would not have pursued this line of conversation without the backup. 'No way will I adhere to such a demand. If you are relevant then I shall name you.'

'We have friends who don't take kindly to us being falsely implicated, especially my brother and cousins.'

I turn to face Montgomery, 'Have the police asked you why you were following me when I visited the churchyard, or asked for your whereabouts when the mysterious person pushed me into the canal?'

They take a step towards me. Their faces are hostile.

I stand my ground. I won't be intimidated. 'Instead of attempting to threaten me. If you didn't kill Jasmine, why don't you help me and the police solve the murder then we can return to our peaceful independent lives where we never speak again.'

Samantha's eyes smoulder with fire and hatred. Montgomery clenches his fists at his side. Before they can reply I turn on my heels and head for the door, 'Let me know guys.'

In haste I stride along the passageway and skip up the steps to the stern deck.'

'Get her.' The screaming voice is full of hatred. 'She's not messing us around any longer.'

Pounding footsteps sound along the passageway. I step up to the towpath and stand between Ryan and Freddie who were waiting for me.

Montgomery and Samantha crash out onto the stern deck. I grin with wicked enjoyment at the bewildered expressions which fills their faces as they spot my two escorts. Surprisingly, they give up their pursuit.

The debrief session is short and to the point, as we all agree that their aggressive behaviour suggests they have something to hide.

47

The doorbell rings at dad's house. I am on my own, but Rufus and Matey kick up a terrible din. I am expecting a friend from the past so I'm not too concerned. Closing the internal passage door on the dogs, I peer through the peephole in the door and confirm my expectation. A friendly faced man with a shock of dark hair greying at the temples stands on the doorstep. It's Clement.

Flinging open the door I greet him with a beaming smile, 'Hi. Thanks for agreeing to come and help.'

Clement, a tall distinguished looking man, points at the door a few feet away with a worried expression. 'They sound big.'

I grin with amusement. 'They are, but they will calm, believe me.' Opening the door, 'Sit.' Matey is always the first to obey but while following instructions, Rufus continues to bark. I touch the top of his head and ruffle his fur. He understands and calms. 'Back away.' They do as instructed, but Rufus keeps looking backwards to eye the newcomer.

'The kitchen table is the centre of operations. The kettle is on and cakes are waiting.' The dogs wander away as they have lost interest.

I pour the coffees and place the cakes on the table.

'You've been in the news a lot recently Amanda. How can I help?'

'The police are close to arresting me for the murder of Jasmine.'

He regards me steadily with a bewildered expression, 'That's not good news. I was amazed when I read the reports of what happened on the boats.' He selects a chocolate chip muffin and silence follows as he enjoys the first taste. After a sip of coffee he continues, 'How is your dad? It's years since we crossed paths on criminal cases. He was a good copper and we got on well.'

'He's okay but is having a check-up at the hospital after he was mugged.'

'Is it connected with the murder case?'

There is no deceiving Clement who has one of the quickest minds I have ever worked with. A former policeman who had become a journalist.

'Dad suggested I try to discover who is committing the crimes as the police are not making progress.'

'Risky business.'

'I have a backup group and we are wired.'

'Good thinking.'

'The victim was Jasmine. In many ways friendly, but I believe she has a hidden side. I have been unable to discover much about her so dad suggested you. With your vast experience, you are the top man in the newspaper industry for finding information people want to stay hidden.'

'Flattery will get you everywhere. Of course, I will help. Give me the details of your progress.'

I pass him the printout of my searches so far. He sets up his laptop. Mine is already on the table.

'What are you researching, Amanda?'

'The killer could well be associated with the boats, so I am checking out each person in turn. Some are relatively easy, such as Benjamin Foster, the author, but others are more difficult.

'Okay, let's settle down and I will give it my best shot.'

An hour later, Clement leans back in his chair. 'It's always difficult to be certain that I have found the right person as she was deliberately elusive and difficult to trace. Would she be likely to have had a criminal record for falsifying documents and embezzlement?

'Possibly. What have you found?'

'Her real name was Ann Jasmine Ruth Brown. She came from Manchester and was sacked and prosecuted by a well-known creative arts company. I've emailed you the full details.'

'Thanks, Clement.'

'Is your dad home soon, I would love to meet him again.'

'Yes, in about half an hour.'

'I presume he has retired.'

'Yes, about ten months ago.'

'What does he do with his spare time. He was always a dedicated copper who spent all working hours on cases.'

'Don't ask.' I chuckle with amusement, 'He has built a model railway, and spends all his waking hours playing and making it more complicated and elaborate as the months pass.'

'Wow. What fun! Will he let me see it?'

'Come on, he doesn't mind people playing with it, I will show you.'

48

Glancing at my phone after Clement has left, I have a text message from Russell. Previously I had given Letitia my phone number who must have passed it on. The text is brief. Ring me.

The team sit around the kitchen table to listen in to the conversation. Freddie will record it all. Placing my phone into speaker mode I press the number that Russell had transmitted.

'Hi Russell, it's Amanda.'

'No time to talk now. I've important information. Will you meet me?'

I look around the table. They all give a thumbs up to indicate their approval.

'Yes, where?' Any dubious building that I don't know might be tricky but I can always suggest an alternative.

'At Shadwell, on the street near the basin. It overlooks the Thames.'

'Near the Prospect of Whitby?'

'Yes. Do you know it?'

I glance across at dad to gauge his reaction, as he will make an instant assessment of the risks. He nods.

'Can you manage eight thirty this evening, as I am leaving the country tomorrow.'

As I stride along the road towards the meeting venue, a few people are coming and going to the pub, but a few hundred yards along the road it is quiet, where the road leaves the waterfront and disappears between warehouses. Freddie has parked his van within sight of the meeting place. Dad and Linda are having a drink in the pub and stand by the door pretending to watch the boats coursing up and down the river.

Russell casually leans on the railings looking out over the Thames. He glances up and notices me but doesn't alter his position and continues to stare out over the river. I step next to him and lean on the railings. Abigail and Ryan pass behind us, holding hands with their hoodies up. Russell doesn't look around.

'I won't tell you where I am going.'

A strange start to a conversation, but he requested the meeting as he wanted to impart information, so I will remain relaxed.

'Why the meet?'

Turning to stare at me, he frowns in a troubled manner, 'Sorry, lass, but I pushed you into the canal.' The admission comes as a surprise. It's probably the reason he's not telling me where he is going. Strangely, I feel no animosity to him.

'Why did you do it?'

'Letitia told me you were causing trouble with Benjamin and the *Green Boat*. In her view, your presence now that Jason has gone will disrupt everyone's life as she considers you to be a troublemaker. She suggested I should think of a way to force you to leave.'

My mind twirls as I think through his words. Why did Letitia want me to leave? Why does she think I am a troublemaker? What have I done to upset her? She appears to have little to do with the people on the other boats. None of Russell's words make sense.

He licks his lips and turns back to the black night view over the Thames. 'Sorry. I assumed you would swim to the bank. But the shock of the push and the impact of the cold water coupled with the restrictions of your clothes caused you to seriously flounder. I might have killed you, but thankfully you were rescued by your dog.'

'If I promise that I will not report you for pushing me into the canal, will you be honest with me?'

He shuffles uncomfortably, but he is far enough away from me that I do not become concerned. 'Okay, but I will admit to nothing.'

Again, a strange stance, but he might be a good source of information so I will start by asking some simple questions.

'Russell, when I visited your boat with Linda, you made a pass at Linda and grabbed a good handful of my bum then invited me for a discreet coffee.'

He wraps his arms about himself and shakes his head slowly from side to side, 'Say sorry to Linda, will you?'

This is a different Russell to the man I have met before but why the change? He gives me a glance waiting for me to continue.

'Yes, I will pass your message to Linda. On *Serendipity,* after I came out of the water, I shed some of my clothes and you wrapped me in towels but did not try to grope me when I was vulnerable.'

He breathes out in several long gasps, 'Without going into details I came under Letitia's influence. She treated me as her errand boy, but she paid the bills and bought me good clothes.' He would not be, as Letitia proclaimed, an engineer working overseas on dams, but I will not pursue that point. 'I wanted to get away from Letitia but that would only work if she kicked me out.'

It is too difficult to think of the implications while he is talking. I can review those with the rest of the team later, so I wait for him to continue.

'In desperation I came up with the idea that if she saw me drooling over other younger women, she would end our relationship.'

'Did you target the women on the nearby boats?'

'Yes, but it was a risky strategy, because I worried about the men beating me up.'

'Tell me everything.' Even in the dark I hear him gulping. 'I don't intend to inform the police that you pushed me in the canal if you furnish me with some information.'

'I don't know what to tell you.'

I am intrigued as Linda and I had endured his attention but who else and more importantly what was their reaction.

'Which women did you try?'

'Samantha was the first.'

My God either he didn't know her, or he was a brave man.

'She stumbled on the towpath in the twilight. I jumped

up to help and squeezed her bum in the process. She slapped my face. I hoped Letitia had observed the incident.'

'What happened?'

'Nothing apart from her parting words. *Don't molest me. Next time ask and the answer might be favourable.*' I am stunned by this snippet of information.

Samantha and Montgomery are a strange couple. A great many questions about them need answering. Why have they been so aggressive towards me? What are they hiding?

The hoodies of Ryan and Abigail drift past again. Abigail giggles. I try to keep a straight face. The two hoody lovers pass by on their slow journey.

'I've told you the truth, will you let me go without calling the police.'

'Yes, one last question. Did you try it with Jasmine.'

'Yes. At a reception on the *Green World* for their business colleagues. You were away at the time.'

I want to bring him back to the topic, 'Jasmine.'

'During a slow dance, I touched her up. *I didn't know you fancied me Russell, why not book somewhere private*. I booked a hotel room but did not expect her to show.'

'Assuming you were meeting for sex, what did she talk about?'

'She was willing to have sex but only wanted to talk about Letitia's paintings.'

As a police patrol car on a routine surveillance, glides past, he turns and sprints away.

49

Shell shocked from the revelations by Russell, I drift along the road to Freddie's van and climb into the back. He has converted it to a makeshift campervan. Linda climbs into the back as well, with dad sliding into the front passenger seat. Abigail and Ryan arrive and join us in the back. It's a little cramped but no one is complaining as we are all too tired.

'After the revelations of today and especially with Russell my brain is addled. It's getting late so shall we review in the morning.'

Dad twists around from the front seat. 'Yes, I agree, it has been a long day.'

We drift into silence. Abigail's voice stirs us from our daydreaming and sleepy thoughts as Freddie drives us home. 'Grandad.'

Dad chuckles as he often does when she wants to ask him a question. 'Yes.'

'When you worked in the police, did you do an operation similar to tonight, with wired earpieces and hidden people?'

'Yes, that is one aspect of police work.'

'But you never knew whether the person would turn violent or have his friends nearby.'

'That's true.'

'Bloody hell, such work is terrifying. I'm doing an office job.'

The laughter from all relaxes the atmosphere and I wrap my arm around Abigail's shoulder and give her a hug.

Approaching nine thirty and anticipating that we have finished for the day I had relaxed on the drive home. As Freddie pulls up in front of the house, 'Someone is sitting on your steps.'

I move so I have a better view, 'It's Benjamin. Sorry guys we haven't finished for the day.' They refix their earpieces. 'Are you okay to record, Freddie?'

'No issue.' He gives a thumbs up and reaches into his

bag. After a few twiddles of the knobs on his equipment, he glances up. 'Ready to go.'

It is brilliant to have such a team behind me. 'I'll take Benjamin to the kitchen and ply him with gin. Shall we all meet in the morning for a debrief?'

Everyone agrees, so Dad leads the way to the door, and I am the last to climb out of the van. As I wander down the path I sing quietly to myself so that Freddie can check the microphones are working correctly. Don't ask me why but I am singing a Beatles song, It's been a Hard day's Night. I glance back at the van and Freddie gives me a thumbs up. I wave. Benjamin will assume I am waving goodbye. Benjamin stands on the doorstep waiting for me with an inane grin. Dad quietens the dogs. Abigail gives Benjamin a cheery hello. Perfect.

'Hi, Benjamin, come in.' I usher him down the hall towards the kitchen. Abigail produces a bottle of gin from the lounge and I procure tonics and ice cubes from the fridge. The noise of movement in the house dissipates and I pour two large gins. With the other people around, he has avoided an embrace and I am not close enough to smell his breath.

His eyes are struggling to focus so he is under the influence of drink or drugs which has been the usual pattern for every meeting recently. 'It's good to see you again, Benjamin. Has there been a development that you have come to tell me about?'

'No, the police have not been back to me since we met, this morning.'

So much has happened today it is hard to believe it was only this morning that I had visited him.

'Is it just a social visit then?'

'I'd love it to be, but you are not interested in a relationship with me, I can tell.'

I make no movement or comment.

'But I want to put a business proposition to you.'

'I'm listening.'

'A rumour came to me today that you no longer work for

the newspaper.'

I slowly move my head to acknowledge his words while keeping a neutral face as far as I can determine.

'Jasmine helped with writing jobs. Basic editing and preparing the manuscripts for the publishers. So, I'm looking for someone else to help me with these activities both in the short and long term. If you would like the job on whatever your current salary was then could we try it for three months?'

'This comes as a surprise, Benjamin.'

I fix a stare on him as I top up the gin. 'Does the job description include sleeping with you as Jasmine did?'

He leans back and laughs. 'I'd love it to include that, but you don't fancy me. So, no it does not and I have a new girlfriend to satisfy my needs.'

After finishing his second drink Benjamin leaves. His departure might have been prompted by my excessive yawning. While I exaggerated, I am tired. It's been a busy day.

Snuggled up in my cosy bed I reflect on Benjamin's visit. The question that repeats itself over and over in my mind is, did he murder Jasmine? He's wasted little time in acquiring himself a new girlfriend so he can't be that heartbroken. I am convinced Jasmine was ghost writing his novels, although he suggested it was just editing and proof reading. I don't believe him. His annoyance at her relationship with Jason was obvious as they intended to split up and move from the boat. On the night of the party when under the influence of excessive drink and drugs, did he exact his revenge on Jasmine? It's a possibility.

Day Eight

50

Although I slept well, I scan through the information we gathered yesterday before I leave the warm comfort of my bed. It had been a busy day. I'd spoken with Benjamin on two occasions, and at both meetings he had been drunk and his eyes showed signs of drug taking. Letitia's reaction to the mention of the Suffolk Coast had been confusing. Why had she lied? Clement's research into Jasmine's background had revealed her criminal record. The altercation on the *Green Boat* with Samantha and Montgomery had indicated their dislike of me. After that the conversation with Russell when he confessed to pushing me in the canal was bewildering. Yes, it had been an eventful day. As I shower, I reflect on the meetings we had completed but come to no conclusions. The breakfast discussion with the others might help to calm my mind as it will set priorities for the way forward.

The coffee filter machine is already hissing and bubbling when I arrive, but the kitchen is empty. Voices reach me from upstairs. I follow the sound and discover dad and Freddie playing with the trainset. They are having fun. Their eyes are alert and their smiles wide. They remind me of two young boys. Shaking my head in amusement I wander back to the kitchen. Linda has baps, sausages and bacon lined up on the work surface.

'Hello, darling.'

A wonderful smile covers her face, so I cross and hug her. 'You've done so well supporting dad and helping me.' I still cannot believe the transformation in the woman that I had known for over twenty years and obviously never understood.

'All the undercover work is so exciting. I haven't enjoyed myself so much in years. Your dad and Freddie keep us all safe. Some of the information I have listened to is quite unbelievable.'

Bleary eyed Abigail comes slouching into the kitchen in her dressing gown. 'Ryan heard the train set and has joined the men, or should I say boys.' I wrap my arms around her. Breaking free she slumps onto a kitchen chair as she rubs her face to dispel the lingering sleepiness. 'What are we doing, guys?'

'Coffees and teas for the railway room followed by sausage and bacon baps, which we will also serve there.'

Abigail, despite not being a morning person, enters into the spirit and organises the mugs on the trays along with the milk jugs and sugar bowl. 'Those conversations we listened to yesterday were amazing. What did you think of them, Gran?'

'I agree, I didn't go to sleep for ages thinking about them.'

Abigail picks up the first trays of mugs. 'I've been so foolish and naïve. I could easily have been conned.'

I frown in puzzlement at her statement as it makes no sense.

Linda puts her arm around Abigail's shoulder. 'How is that related to the conversations?'

She places the tray of mugs down. 'I got on well with Jasmine and liked her dress sense. We laughed and joked about men. Although she was a lot older than me, I thought her a kindred spirit. It shattered my impression of her when I found out about the affair with dad, but yesterday was unbelievable. She slept with the men in every boat! It's too much to think about at this time in the morning.' She picks up the tray again as Linda and I laugh.

Armed with breakfast we venture up to the railway room. The three men are intently focused. Abigail shakes her head. 'If we need to rely on these three, it will be a hopeless cause, just look at them.'

Dad glances across at us as we stand gawping. 'Linda you can have the Intercity. It's that control box.' He points.

Abigail pushes out her bottom lip pretending to pout but has a twinkle in her eye, 'I'm not playing unless I can have the Flying Scotsman.'

'That control box.'

'What's left for me?' The enthusiasm in the room lifts my spirits and I grin.

'The shunting yard.'

Everyone abandons their controls and picks up a breakfast bap plus a tea or coffee.

Laughter percolates the room as we have our food and drinks and play with the trains. Our laughter is mingled with the hooting, whistling and rattling which emanates from the trains as they speed around the track. It seems a pity to draw the fun to an end, but I keep jumping back to the meetings yesterday, some of which were serious and need a resolution. 'Guys, can we sort out a plan for today? I need your input as I don't know where to start.'

The trains gradually come to a halt.

Dad's face lights up with a mischievous grin, 'The plan is obvious, isn't it.'

I giggle at his enthusiasm but shake my head. Abigail and Linda both shrug and appear bewildered. Ryan studies dad with a bemused expression.

Dad carries on grinning, 'What do you think, Freddie?'

'Perfectly obvious plan.'

I laugh in genuine amusement, 'What a wicked pair you are. Come on. Give us all a clue.'

'Freddie and I put our heads together earlier this morning. The same listening is not needed for today as we can ensure everyone's safety. Freddie and I will meet with Clement and deal with the *Green Boat*. They were nasty yesterday and Samantha has a temper. We are going to delve into their background and if necessary, confront them with an investigative article about some topic we uncover.'

'Charles,' Linda stares at dad and raises her eyebrows in a questioning manner. 'Is my best ploy to deal with my son. He holds no threats to me and has a lot of explaining to do. As I am his only current source of money, I shall bribe the truth out of him.'

My eyes open wide at Linda. The steeliness in her voice highlights her determination.

Freddie puts his thumb up to Linda, 'That's what we thought as well.'

'Abigail, are you feeling brave?'

'Dad, perhaps you should not involve Abigail directly.'

'Shush, mum.'

I am being organised, so I slump back in my seat and listen.

'Grandad, what do you want me to do?'

'Benjamin is looking for someone to help with formatting his manuscripts. Go with Ryan who has read Benjamin's books and talk about Jasmine. He is much more likely to let information slip to you as you were with Jasmine many times.'

I shudder as I do not like the idea of Abigail visiting Benjamin. Should I intervene after this meeting and persuade her to drop the issue.

'Good idea, grandad.'

'I agree, sir. He will be relaxed talking about his books.' For once, Ryan gives a broad smile. The two young lovers exchange a brief kiss.

I will have no chance of dissuading them.

'That only leaves me. Do you want me to revisit Letitia?'

'Yes and do some follow up research about Jasmine. From your newspaper connections have you a specialist art gallery that could advise you about their work and paintings.'

'Yes.'

'Remember no walking around. Use taxis, otherwise stay at home with Rufus and Matey.'

Linda flicks her hand in the air, 'What about Russell?'

Dad glances at Freddie who nods. 'Good point, Linda. Russell will be the most difficult one to trace and find out further information about, but we suspect he is not a threat. We will include him in our conversation with Clement.'

I put my head on one side, 'How do you come to the conclusion that he is not a threat?'

Your conversation with him. I ran it through the lie detector. At no point during yesterday's discussion with you did he lie. We suspect he is a small-time con artist. Russell is not likely to be his real name. The trip to build a dam might well have been time he spent in jail. Whoever he is, he believed Letitia had a hold over him and if Letitia did, and remember, he showed no signs of lying, what is the connection. Both con artists?

Dad glances at his watch. 'Breakfast was early. It is only just after eight. What about another half hour with the trains before we embark on the day.' A cheer erupts and I settle to moving the shunting engine backwards and forwards connecting trucks and depositing them in different sidings to await the arrival of the freight engine. Whistling, hooting and laughter fill the air.

51

The dour man, Mr Green, sitting behind the desk stands to greet me, but there is no smile. Small, balding and with a dark grey suit he is everything I expect of an art expert from a top London gallery. Half glasses are on the desk next to his fountain pen. In a slow and precise manner, he puts them on. Why does he do that as he now peers at me over the top of them?

'How may I help you?' He glances at the appointment schedule on his desk, 'Mrs Mallory.'

But I have dealt with such experts before, and they need softening up. It might require a little time before the penny drops. This amuses me. I smile in an ingratiating manner. A little voice in my head whispers, tell me what I want to know, or I shall write the most damming article about your gallery. However, we have a long way to go before we reach that stage.

Opening my handbag, I flash my press card. 'I am a freelance journalist and wish to start a series about relatively unknown but living landscape artists. My initial ideas will be to focus on artists who favour coastal scenes. Do you think that might be an interesting topic?'

Although I am preaching to the converted, I am attempting to encourage him to talk.

He rests his elbows on the table and steeples his fingers, 'An interesting theme in which there are many talented artists.'

He is warming to me as his life revolves around art and he enjoys demonstrating his expertise. 'I would perceive the articles as relating the painting to the painter especially if they were local to that environment.'

He presses a buzzer on the intercom. 'Two coffees, please.'

'Thank you. Can you name the top four?'

He purses his lips. He is in his element. 'I will write them down for you.'

The coffee arrives. It is all neatly laid out on a tray. Everything is coordinated. It looks posh. I pour my coffee and cream into a Wedgewood cup with matching saucer. A warning voice in my head reminds me to be careful.

He hands me the list. I glance down it. Only one name I recognise from my search of the web in the taxi on the way here.

'Ah, I am pleased you have included Justin Tremlins. His pictures of the Norfolk Broads are amongst my favourites.

He smiles in a more friendly manner. I'm amused but don't allow my expression to change. Got you, my man. While he would dismiss me as an amateur, the four he has recommended would bring his gallery substantial commission as their prices would go up if featured in a popular newspaper. Although he had sacked me, Toby would accept an article from me on a freelance basis.

'Thank you, Mr Green. I assume you would have no objections to a positive mention in the article of your expertise.'

He dips his head in acknowledgement.

'Perhaps you could help me with two artists who claim to be rising to a breakthrough but your opinion will be valuable to me.'

'Yes, if I am familiar with their work.'

'Letitia Harris.'

He frowns in a disapproving manner causing the lines on his forehead to deepen. 'Not so good.'

'At least you have heard of her.'

'Her paintings can be valued between one and two thousand. Not much originality and sticks to old methods too religiously but has good composition.'

'Do you act as her agent?'

He shakes his head.

'Would you be prepared to tell me the name of her artistic agent so that I may arrange an interview with her?'

'Yes, Mr Russell King, here is his telephone number.'

I am astounded at making such quick progress.

'The other artist is a much younger woman who was painting as I passed by the other day along the coastal path in

Suffolk. I became interested as I was thinking about this article. She was with many friends and I only caught her name as Jasmine but one of her friends wrote her full name down for me.' I pass him the note that Clement had given me with Jasmine's full name.

'I don't recognise the name, but she may sign her pictures with an abbreviated version. Did she say whether she was an amateur?'

'No. That is why I asked you. She mentioned her paintings sold between one and two thousand.'

I have caught his interest again.

'Would you allow me to use my computer?'

'Please do.'

He slips a large tablet computer from his top drawer. 'Yes, I have found the reference. They are sold for between one and two thousand pounds and are coastal or traditional water scenes in East Anglia. They are signed JR which from the note you have given me is her middle two initials.

'Thank you.'

He is distracted. He shuffles in his seat and no longer maintains eye contact. After carefully storing his computer back into the drawer. He raises his head, 'Interesting. The comparison between the two artists is unusual.'

'Can you elaborate, Mr Green?'

'Sorry, only gallery musings.' He flaps his hand in a dismissive gesture and rises from his seat. 'Let me show you out and I hope our gallery may receive a mention.'

52

Stepping from the taxi outside dad's home, I glance around out of habit. With no one in the street, I flit up the step to the front door and insert the key. The barking welcomes me home. A sigh of relief escapes from my lips. Those two will be my protectors until the others arrive as I expect I am first to return.

Abigail appears from the kitchen, scampers along the hallway and wraps her arms around me in an enthusiastic gesture. 'Mum, you must listen to our meeting with Benjamin. It was a disaster!' She grips my arm and ushers me along the hall to the kitchen where Ryan sits at the kitchen table.

'Calm down, darling.' Although I'm anxious to hear what happened her flushed and worried face concerns me.

Ryan places a coffee in front of me. He has a grim face. Even grimmer than usual.

I move my hands in a pacifying motion. 'Take it slowly, Abigail.'

Settling herself, she inhales deeply and has a sip of coffee. 'When he opened the door, I could tell the meeting would not go well. Normally he has always greeted me with a smile and a hug, but he gave us no word of greeting and walked away from the door expecting us to follow him.'

Without speaking he indicated for us to sit on the settee. He didn't sit but stood glowering at us.

'Your mother is an interfering cow and if she ever mentions the information, she gleaned from the publisher to anyone else, she needs to be very wary of me.'

Abigail studies my face before continuing, 'While I didn't like his aggressive tone, I assumed that he had misinterpreted an incident, so I asked what had upset him. He snarled, *'She has suggested that my novels were written by Jasmine and not me. My publisher took a lot of persuading early this morning that I wrote them and Jasmine was only the formatter.* At that point, a woman came into the room. In her twenties, she was tall and slim with long blonde hair.'

The publisher must have had doubts after our meeting and checked on the manuscripts. He would have been able to get expert advice about the writing and must have concluded that the style was sufficiently different to warrant tackling Benjamin about it.

He waved an accusing finger towards us, *'Abigail is the daughter of the conniving, secretive woman who I told you about this morning. These two are leaving. I no longer want them in my flat as they have connections with Amanda.* It was scary as I have never seen him so aggressive.'

'Did you leave?'

'Yes. The woman escorted us to the front door, and shouted after us as we walked away, *'I hope Benjamin gets revenge on your mother as he has threatened.'*

Benjamin's actions reveal that Jasmine was the author of the recent novel. Had she assumed responsibility and produced the book which is destined to be a best seller. It would have been about the time for her to demand more payment. Or perhaps she decided to filch the money, as she had embezzlement skills. Either way he had a motive to murder her because, if she went public, he would lose his income and credibility.

Ryan has remained silent as Abigail related the story. He tops up the coffee from the filter machine. 'I spoke with Freddie before we left this house and we recorded the interview.'

'Thanks, Ryan. You are a star.'

'I did not like the aggression in his face when he talked about you.'

The sound of the dogs barking indicate someone else has arrived. Linda comes into the kitchen and drops into a chair. Her face is flushed and her hand trembles as she sips the coffee that Ryan had given her.

'Are you okay, Linda?'

Pressing her lips together she gulps in a deep breath, 'Yes, I'm calming but I had an almighty row with Jason.'

'Wasn't he prepared to understand reason?'

'I'm afraid he needs serious help. I told him so as he was drunk and it was only ten o'clock in the morning. Unfortunately, I didn't prepare myself for the meeting. In retrospect I should have thought it through in more detail. He became aggressive and I am afraid, it does not happen very often, but I lost my temper and we had a shouting match.'

Linda has to put her coffee down as her hand is shaking violently. I catch her hand to try to reassure her as it must have been a terrible ordeal. Abigail leaps up and hugs her around her shoulders. 'Please calm down, Gran.'

'Thank you darling it's good to be with friends and the people I love.'

'Just relax. You don't have to tell us the details if you prefer not.'

She clutches my hand in both of hers. 'At one time in the meeting he threatened to hit me.'

Tears stream down her face.

'Linda, you poor soul.' My words sound inadequate as the confrontation must have been traumatic. This is terrible. What has happened to Jason? Linda does not deserve such treatment as she has always been supportive towards her only son.

After gulping a few times, 'I want to tell you.'

'Okay, take it slowly.'

'I challenged him and would not back down when he threatened to hit me. *Are you going to hit your mother, the same as you have hit your wife. And you have done it a second time since we spoke about it.*

That cow told the police and I have been arrested and cautioned because of her but that won't stop me. I intend making her give me half of all our money. She owes and she will pay, regardless of the police.'

We have calmed Linda to some extent but the meeting with Jason must be replaying through her mind over and over again. I must ensure in the weeks ahead that she has the support she requires. By lunchtime the threats from the morning are beginning to overwhelm me, but it is my duty to remain positive as both Linda and Abigail have been shaken by their morning experience.

The barking indicates that dad and Freddie have returned. I prepare a serving plate full of sandwiches for everyone. I make plenty as Freddie has a healthy appetite. As Abigail and Linda repeat their events of the morning, I place the sandwiches in the middle of the kitchen table, 'How did you get on dad?'

'We had a meeting with Clement to research into those on the *Green World*, but it was soon pushed aside by other events as we then met the police. The details of the meetings are not important, only the information that came out of them.

Silence settles on the kitchen as Dad and Freddie help themselves to food. We wait expectantly. '*Green World* has recently come to the attention of the drugs squad. The enquiries are still in the initial stages but they are focusing their attention on a coffee shop which is thought to be a meeting place.'

'Dad, is it in Paddington near the station?'

Both Freddie and Dad stare at me with surprise.

'When I sorted out Jasmine's clothes, I found several receipts for a coffee shop in Paddington.'

'There is a reason to believe that the drugs suspicions are well founded as when the police went to pick up Montgomery and Samantha they have disappeared and have not been sighted since yesterday. They had important meetings at their work, but they did not turn up. Their clothes and personal possessions have disappeared from *Green World*.

With the plates cleared the kitchen falls silent. Everyone is engrossed in their own thoughts. The reported issues have enveloped those in the kitchen with a chilly tension.

'Grandad?'

He blinks rapidly to return to the present, pushing his thoughts aside. 'Yes, Abigail.'

'Mum is being threatened from all angles and Grandma is not safe unless she is with Ryan and Freddie who can protect her. Do we tell the police everything we know and then will they arrest everyone.'

Both Dad and Freddie shake their heads. Freddie leans forward and smiles reassuringly at Abigail. 'While the police will interview the people there would be little in the way of charges and it will not solve the key problem of the murder.'

Abigail flaps her hands. Her agitation is palpable. 'Yes, I understand, but we must do something we cannot just sit waiting for an attack as everyone must soon return to their normal lives which are isolated from each other.'

Freddie glances at her in warm acknowledgement, 'That is a good reading of the situation. One potential solution springs to mind.' He glances at dad.

'Yes, but not Amanda.'

'I agree, it's me.'

'I'd prefer you and Ryan.'

Despite the tension I have to smile, 'Will you please explain to us mortals what you two are talking about, as I have no idea?'

'You will return to the boat this afternoon. We will be nearby, but I don't expect any activity until after dark. If anyone is watching, we will be hidden. If they notice you arriving at the boat, the person might return after dark. As night falls, you will leave the boat and join the surveillance party. Freddie and Ryan will take your place. Then we wait.'

A worrying frown settles on Linda's face, 'Isn't it too dangerous to try to flush them out?'

Freddie grins, 'Don't worry Linda. We will install extra remote-control lights. If Charles hears or observes anything he doesn't like from the stakeout he will turn on the lights, use a loudspeaker system set up in the van and let the dogs loose.'

Linda and I open our eyes in amazement at the instantaneous planning that has happened.

53

Despite dad's attempt to persuade Linda and Abigail not to be involved they are adamant they want to be there. Finally, it is agreed they will have a minor role to perform but then they will be in the car at the top of the footpath where the police caravan had been parked. They will have a view from there over the canal.

In the late afternoon, I return to the boat with Freddie who carries a heavy bag. If anyone notices it looks as though he is carrying it for me. The strong north wind sends the shivers down my back but not only from the weather but also being involved in a stakeout although I will not be in a position to be threatened. I have checked several times with Ryan that he agrees to be involved. As undemonstrative as when I had first met him, he assures me he fully approves of the plan.

As we approach the stern of *Serendipity,* I spot a bottle near the locked entrance to the boat. Freddie steps forward, 'I'll lead until we are certain what it is?'

I delay stepping onto the boat. He beckons me forward as he picks up the bottle of gin. 'The label has part of the corner missing but the seal on the bottle is fine.'

'What does the card say?'

He tears away the card from the neck of the bottle, 'My apologies.'

'Any name?'

'No. The label is printed so there is no clue in the handwriting.'

Freddie places the lights on the stern and in the bow. They look no different to lights on many boats, then with a cheery wave of his hand he walks away along the towpath. Meandering through the boat I will tidy, dust and air the space as it has been closed up for long periods over recent days. Nervousness grips me but I have tested the radio connections and they are working well, but we agreed on radio silence after testing.

Will someone come for me?

If so, who will it be?

I shake my head although no one can see me. How have I made enemies of people who were my neighbours? Too much thinking will be my own downfall.

As dusk settles with a minor amount of mist on the canal, dad's voice sounds on the radio. 'Time to swap. Leave the internal boats lights on. Two hoodies with a bright lantern will come along the towpath to capture people's attention by playing loud music.'

I recognise the giggles from Abigail and Linda in the background.

'When they are level with *Green World, Serendipity* will be in darkness. Slip out go up the path and around the long way to the van. Freddie and Ryan will come along and board the boat. Before we put the plan into action can you perform a small task?'

'Yes, dad. What is it?'

'The bottle that was delivered to the boat today. Do not touch the contents but pour half of it down the sink and place it on the dinette table with the label facing the door.'

I want to ask why but suspect I will not receive an answer, so I comply and then put on my long black anorak.

'Bottle of gin in place and I'm ready to go.'

'Good girl. Away you go, ladies.'

Distant music sounds. Glancing in the direction of Regent's Park along the towpath a bright light appears. The black clad figures with hoods up move slowly. Dad will have given them specific instructions.

My stomach flips somersaults. There is no danger to me or the others. Dad is watching from the van settled somewhere in the blackness. The slightest hint of danger to any of us and he will release the dogs which will come to whoever calls. Rufus coming through the dark will be a terrifying sight for the assailant.

The music becomes louder as they reached *Serendipity*. The bright light dims everything into blackness that's not within its halo. They pass on.

A dog walker advances in the opposite direction. 'Wait, Linda, Abigail. Wait, Amanda.'

They stop and I hover by the doorway to the stern deck.

'Go!'

I skip up to the towpath and half run to the footpath and bound up it as the two darkened figures arrived at *Serendipity*.

We are set for what could be a long evening without a productive result. Dad and Freddie are confident something will happen, but I do not share their optimism.

54

The whisper from dad in the driver's seat wakes me just after one o'clock as I have been sleeping on the bench seat in Freddie's van with the dogs on the floor next to me. 'A figure, dressed in black is hovering near the back of *Serendipity* looking around. Too difficult to discern size and shape.'

Freddie gives an immediate reply, 'Main bedroom, ready.'

Ryan's voice follows, 'Second bedroom, ready.'

I peer from the back of the van but cannot identify the shadowy figure.'

'Get ready, Amanda. You will be quicker than me. Wake the dogs.'

I move to the back door of the van.

'Figure is stepping to the stern deck. We are on.'

'Check.'

'Check.'

The men on the boat were ready.

'Entering the dining area.'

'Go! Go!'

'Assailant has a knife, put the knife down.' Freddie's voice sounds calm. I race to the boat and jump on to the stern deck. As I regain my balance, Rufus shoots past me into the dining area. As if he knew, he takes a flying leap at the wrist of the hand holding the knife. The scream is penetrating, as the knife clatters to the floor. Rufus's heavy body makes contact, poleaxing the intruder to the floor.

The two men pounce and pin the person down with no chance of them escaping. Dad, Abigail and Linda arrive. Freddie wrenches the anorak hood back and pulls a balaclava from over the head. He grins.

I step forward, 'Welcome to my family and friends, Letitia.'

'You were supposed to drown because of too much gin. I deliberately bought a bottle that was high strength. A couple of those and you wouldn't have been able to stand. Jasmine would not give up being nosey and asking questions and then you started. Keep that bloody dog away from me he has broken my wrist.'

'Tough, he stays until the police arrive.'

55

It is good to return to a normal life again. I control the dogs as Abigail answers the front door at Dad's house. She doesn't smile at the person standing in the porch.

'Good evening, Constable Smith.' Her voice is far from welcoming.

The dogs recognise him and both drop to sitting and stop barking.

Abigail frowns with an air of hostility, 'I suppose you'd better come in, although your actions in the past have been unacceptable. You tried to arrest my mother for murder.'

I laugh, but Abigail is showing no signs of mellowing in his presence.

'I've come to update you on police activities since the arrest of Letitia.'

Abigail points, 'This way. We are upstairs. I suppose as you are a guest bringing helpful news, I will have to let you have the Flying Scotsman and as you are a boy you won't be able to resist.'

Constable Smith's face crinkles with confusion as he stares at me as though hoping for an explanation.

I chuckle, but don't elaborate, 'You'll see.'

Abigail leads him upstairs into the train room.

'Wow.'

She points, 'Sit there, that is the controller for the Flying Scotsman. It is in the far station, over there. Don't go too fast, granddad does not like people who crash his trains.'

Abigail drifts to the far side of the room and the new extension, that dad has recently begun and sits next to Ryan who is building a mountain railway with the help of Freddie.

As Constable Smith settles, he waves to the others, 'Evening, all. I've come to update Mrs Mallory on the police activities.'

Feeling relaxed at his presence, I smile at him, 'Can you tell the others as well as they were part of the solution.'

'Yes.' We wait as he slowly moves the controller and satisfied the Flying Scotsman was leaving the station, he extracts his notebook from an inside pocket and flips it open.

'As you passed on the tapes that you recorded, they helped us bring many of the issues to a quick conclusion. I will go through each of the boats in turn. Benjamin on *Carpe Diem* has settled his dispute with the publisher after admitting that Jasmine wrote the past three novels. He also discovered the Jasmine had been embezzling from his account.'

Constable Smith peers at the Flying Scotsman which is no longer hurtling around the track. Abigail giggles, 'I've assumed control of the signals and I've stopped you.

He laughs, and looks at me, 'I don't think your daughter likes me.'

'There you are. You can go again.' Abigail grins mischievously.

Dad moves away from the track and relaxes in a chair allowing the others to play, 'What about *Green World*.'

'Drug importers, performed by manipulating their company's tea products. Samantha and Montgomery were captured at Harwich trying to leave the country.'

Linda draws in a deep breath but her forehead is creased with lines of worry, 'Any news on my son?'

He nods, 'He was arrested and cautioned but we judged he needed help with his alcoholism. He wanted to leave London so a volunteer group took him to Birmingham and to a refuge.'

Linda sighs, 'That is the best news I could expect given the circumstances.'

He turns to face me, 'Sorry Mrs Mallory but we judged that prosecuting him for the assault on you which he admitted would not be in the public interest.'

Tears fill my eyes as the image of Jason in his wedding suit appears in my mind. I mop them up and receive a cuddle from Abigail. While the news is devastating, I didn't want him to be charged with assaulting me. He needs help to get his life back on track. Perhaps in the future we might become friends but I no longer want him in my life. 'Thank you for the update.'

Freddie relaxes back in his chair, 'That only leaves the *Kingfisher* boat.'

Constable Smith nods, 'Alfred Sidebottom.'

I guess who he is referring to, but Abigail interrupts, 'Who's he?'

The officer smiles at her although she will not relax her frown, 'You knew him as Russell King. He returned to this country when the murder charges against Letitia were made. That is not her real name. Alfred explained about her forgeries. It appears that although she painted coastal scenes, she was successful at completing copies of popular paintings from the past. The forgeries were sold for substantial sums of money.'

He turns to face me, 'After your visit to the art dealers, the gentlemen you met spotted the similarities between Letitia and Jasmine's work. Jasmine had stolen her paintings and put finishing touches to them and sold them as her own. From his investigations several forgeries were also revealed that had been completed by Jasmine. While her own paintings sold for about two thousand pounds her forgeries would earn over ten thousand each.'

The Constable brings the Flying Scotsman to a halt in the station from where he first started. 'Your press colleague discovered Jasmine's real name. Although prosecuted and imprisoned in Manchester, her life of crime continued. To embezzlement and false representation, she also added blackmail. After stealing the paintings, she threatened Letitia with exposure. But she chose the wrong person in Letitia who has admitted responsibility for her murder.'

Only one further question came to mind, 'What about the original death threat sent to the newspaper about me?'

'Although the police did not view it seriously in the first instance given the other developments, we traced the individual. A special needs man associated with the church in the article who enjoys watching police cars. He is harmless.'

We all breathe a sigh of relief and turn out attention

back to the trains. Whistling, chugging and laughter soon fill the air.

THE END

Enjoy this book?

Thank you for reading my book. If you have time I would appreciate a rating or review. They are a great help to me in developing and writing my books.
You can find more information about my books on my website:

T M Goble's Website

www.tmgoble.com

Action Thrillers
Detective Murder Mysteries
Standalone Murder Mysteries
Historical Fiction
Contemporary Fiction
History of Peak District Literature
Seasonal Recipes
I occasionally send newsletters with details on new releases, special offers and other bits of news relating to my books.

Printed in Great Britain
by Amazon

41477197R00121